WORLD IN DUPLICATE

THE GOLDEN AMAZON SAGA

WORLD IN DUPLICATE

THE GOLDEN AMAZON SAGA, BOOK FIFTEEN

JOHN RUSSELL FEARN

Edited by Philip Harbottle

THE BORGO PRESS

MMXIV

WORLD IN DUPLICATE

FIRST BORGO PRESS EDITION

Published by Wildside Press LLC

www.wildsidebooks.com

CONTENTS

THE GOLDEN AMAZON
by Philip Harbottle

In 1943 British writer John Russell Fearn decided
to quit writing for the American pulp science fiction
magazines, and to concentrate instead on books for the
English market. Within a very few years he became
established as a leading novelist in several genres, not
only science fiction, but also mystery and detective
fiction, and westerns.

His first new SF novel, *The Golden Amazon*, was
published by World's Work in April 1944. In this story,
a little girl of three years of age is made the subject of
an idealistic scientist's illegal glandular experiments.
The scientist's dream is to end world wars by creating
a woman devoid of the usual lusts and frailties of
mankind, who upon reaching maturity would institute
a benign scientific rule. But the apparently successful
experiment has a flaw: it instills into the girl a hatred for
all men, and a ruthless cruelty. Her supernatural scientific gifts enable her to master atomic power, and practically leads her to destroy the world. She breaks the
will and strength of men, and elevates women to positions of wealth and power. She also discovers human

synthesis, and by this means she is able to escape retribution when she is eventually overthrown. She is seen to collapse and die, a victim of consuming ketabolism, echoing the memorable finale of Rider Haggard's *She*. In actuality, it was only her synthetic image, and this paved the way for the *Golden Amazon Returns*, and further sequels

Fearn sold reprint rights in the first novel to the prestigious Canadian magazine, the Toronto *Star Weekly*. The magazine carried a special Comics Supplement, the centre section of which was a 'complete novel', published in newspaper format. Aimed at a general readership, the novels were written by the top popular novelists of the day, including John Dickson Carr, Ellery Queen, and P. G. Wodehouse. They sold hundreds of thousands of copies, and the novels were syndicated to several American newspapers in the Maine and New York areas. The Amazon novels enjoyed extraordinary popularity (especially with Canadian housewives), and ran for the next sixteen years following the appearance of the first novel in the March 3, 1945 issue, ending with Fearn's sudden death in September 1960, aged only fifty-two. His final two Amazon novels appeared posthumously.

During Fearn's lifetime, only the first six novels were published in British hardcover editions from the World's Work in England, after appearing in the *Star Weekly*. This was because the publishers discontinued their entire fiction line in 1954. However, the Amazon novels continued to appear in the *Star Weekly*, eventually notching up twenty-four titles.

Fearn had resold paperback rights to the Canadian publisher Harlequin Books, but after publishing only the first three titles, they stopped publishing SF and other genre fiction to concentrate on their famous Romances line.

Meanwhile, as early as 1949, Fearn had realized that the Amazon series had the potential to run indefinitely. This presented him with a problem, however. The 'origin story' of the Golden Amazon was conceived and actually set during the Second World War. Subsequent novels were written during the war and the immediate postwar period, and projected their stories only a few decades into the future.

He very astutely realized that to keep ahead of reality, he needed to move the Amazon *further* into the future—first into the outer solar system, and thence to the stars. So with the seventh novel, he introduced a new main character, Abna of Atlantis—someone as equally intelligent, and even stronger than herself. These dynamics provided him with an *interstellar* canvas, thus ensuring that the series would remain ahead of reality.

Fearn's strategy was a great success, and the Amazon novels retained their popularity, ending only with his tragically early death in 1960. By then he had written a further twenty Amazon novels, and made preliminary notes for his next (which would later be written by Fearn's biographer, Philip Harbottle).

Long after Fearn's death, his entire Amazon series

would eventually see print from the pioneering US small press Gryphon Books in limited paperback editions, and later by the Canadian Battered Silicon Dispatch Box small press in their hardcover Omnibus series.

This new Borgo Press paperback series will be the first trade edition of all twenty-one of these later novels by Fearn, beginning with the seventh novel in the original series. First published in 1949 as *Conquest of the Amazon*, I have edited it slightly as *World Beneath Ice* (The Golden Amazon Saga, Book One) so that it can be read and enjoyed by new readers who may be totally unfamiliar with what had gone before. Subsequent novels have also been slightly edited for modern readers.

The publishers hope that this new series may create many more "fans of the Amazon." Meanwhile, any reader interested in seeking out the earlier six Golden Amazon novels will find that they are readily available on the internet, and in numerous earlier paperback and hardcover editions.

* * * *

To date, readers can enjoy the following new Borgo Press editions:

Book One: *World Beneath Ice*

In destroying the threat of an alien invasion, the Golden Amazon had inadvertently caused a decline in the sun's heat, encasing Earth in an ice sheet that threatens to eliminate humanity. The Amazon encounters Abna, a descendant of Atlantis, stronger and even more scientifically advanced than she, and the ruler of an Atlantean colony still surviving in a protected environment on Jupiter. She refuses his offer of marriage, but agrees to form an alliance in order to restore the sun and save the Earth. One thing that Abna has not told the Amazon is that all the females of his race have been wiped out by a bacilli infection....

Book Two: *Lord of Atlantis*

A gigantic ridge of land rises from the Atlantic floor, causing massive tidal waves on either side of the ocean. Even stranger, both England and America are then assailed by an invasion of prehistoric monsters! A gigantic domed city rests on the newly risen plateau, whilst out in space an alien spacecraft orbits the Earth. Such are the mysteries and challenges facing the Golden Amazon, self-appointed governess of Earth, as she struggles to unravel the maze of mystery that was the deadly legacy of Atlantis!

Book Three: *Triangle of Power*

The marriage of Violet Ray Brant—better known as The Golden Amazon—and Abna of Atlantis should have ushered in an era of peace and scientific prosperity to the people of Earth. But an unexpected turn of events finds Abna betrayed and marooned on a satellite of Jupiter, and the Amazon flung far beyond the

Solar System. With Earth's two protectors removed, the planet is now at the mercy of another Atlantean, the master scientist Sefner Quorne....

Book Four: *The Amethyst City*

The metaphysical union of the Amazon and Abna results in the mental creation of a fully mature daughter—Viona. Quorne, still struggling for domination, forces Viona into a marriage ceremony, and impregnates her. But with the intervention of Tarnec Brodix, a super-mind from an external universe, Quorne and Viona are separately flung into an ultra-dimensional limbo. Abna chooses to follow after his daughter, leaving the Amazon to brood over the disaster, alone in the Amethyst City of Saturn.

Book Five: *Daughter of the Amazon*

A miscalculation by the super-mathematician Tarnec Brodix destroys his universe, and the fault spreads into the Earth universe in the form of a Dark Tide of Absolute Nothingness. Unable to save himself, Brodix transfers his knowledge into the one mind powerful enough to receive it: that if Sefian, the son who has been born to Viona and Quorne. Sefian rapidly evolves, and, no longer human, after saving the Earth universe, vanishes into the greater universe, to seek new challenges. Then the Amazon is confronted with a further puzzle—a large section of the planet Neptune is discovered to be an exact duplicate of the Earth!

Book Six: *Quorne Returns*

The bacterial intelligences of Neptune plan to conquer Earth by replacing humans in key positions with alien duplicates. The Neptunians are themselves subjugated by the sinister Atlantean scientist, Sefner Quorne. Alerted to the threat, the Golden Amazon hits back by creating the ultimate doomsday weapon—only to precipitate a reprisal from the denizens of another universe....

Book Seven: *The Central Intelligence*

The Golden Amazon's arch-enemy, Sefner Quorne, discovers that all mental gifts, such as memory and creativity, are something that is broadcast throughout the universe by a Central Intelligence—and then interpreted according to the quality of the individual brain of the recipient. At the surprising suggestion of his wife, Viona, the Amazon's daughter, Quorne travels with her to the very center of the universe, in order to wrest the secrets of mentality from the very source itself!

Book Eight: *The Cosmic Crusaders*

The Golden Amazon renounces all ties with Earth when, together with her husband, Abna, and her daughter, Viona, she sets off on a journey to explore the cosmos. On the strange worlds of Alpha Centauri, she encounters Mizanu, the embodiment of evil—a planet-sized hypertrophied brain! Its baleful, crushing mental power threatens to reach out beyond the double-system of Alpha and Proxima Centauri to engulf the Earth and all the other inhabited planets of the galaxy—unless the Amazon can destroy it first!

Book Nine: *Parasite Planet*

The Cosmic Crusaders discover a fantastic world of mental parasites drawing form and substance from our own Earth, fifty light years distant. The planet is ruled by a being identical to the Golden Amazon herself— but an Amazon who's coldly scientific and vicious, mirroring the original Amazon as she had once been early in her career. Inevitably, they become locked in a deadly duel—to the death!

Book Ten: *World Out of Step*

The Cosmic Crusaders find themselves on a planet that seems mysteriously not to conform with natural law, a world out of step with the universe. It leaps ahead into time at unexpected moments, thereby suddenly adding many years of age to the flower-like inhabitants, and killing tens of thousands of individuals through death and old age. In trying to find the alien menace responsible, The Golden Amazon and her fellow Crusaders are flung backwards and forwards through time and space, threatening their own survival....

Book Eleven: *The Shadow People*

The Cosmic Crusaders discover a planet whose people are subject to a baleful influence from outer space that sweeps across their world—and for a brief while embraces every man, woman and child. It stirs the emotions of the sexes against each other. Men desire only to destroy women, and women men. Only those with higher types of mind are able to build a resistance against it. The struggle is dire and dreadful, and leaves its victims physical and mental wrecks. The less fortunate are left dead after the Wave has passed.

But when the Crusaders identify and destroy the source of the problem, they precipitate an even greater menace....

Book Twelve: *Kingpin Planet*

The Cosmic Crusaders are plunged into a strange new space, where all the probabilities of electronic law were strangely altered, a complete and stunning inversion of the so-called natural laws. They discover the mysterious silver planet of Tuca, and deep below its surface they find an enigmatic machine—the legacy of a vanished race. Masters of science, they had overreached themselves by constructing a strange machine that could alter the very laws of nature and electronic probability. The machine had ultimately destroyed them, and blasted a neighboring planet into a cosmic cinder—and unless the Cosmic Crusaders can stop it, it may well destroy the entire universe!

Book Thirteen: *World in Reverse*

Continuing their cosmic crusade amongst the stars, the Golden Amazon and her companions discover a planet in another space where living beings are being synthetically created. The mystery deepens with the discovery that the synthetic race is evolving backwards! Determined to solve these mysteries, the Crusaders find themselves up against the Mithons, a sadistic alien race led by a being known as the Supreme One. Can the Amazon save the day?

Book Fourteen: *Dwellers in Darkness*

Voyaging into a sector of interstellar space plunged into total darkness, the Cosmic Crusaders encounter a powerful and sinister mastermind, who is regarded as a God by the race he has forced to evolve without eyes. And not content with shaping the evolution of their bodies, the mastermind has also impressed on their minds an urge to conquer and dominate...

CHAPTER ONE
THE TRANSPORTED PLANET

The exquisite woman in the black tights, a golden, jewel-studded instrument belt about her waist, sat in deep thought. Again she referred to the photographic prints on the bench before her, studying them intently beneath the bright light. Finally she made several mathematical computations, contemplated them, and then relaxed.

"It just couldn't be," she murmured. "It's at variance with all the laws of celestial mechanics."

Getting to her feet, she crossed to the observation window of the spaceship *Ultra* and, shading the glass from the lights inside the control room, peered intently on to the depths of infinity.

Everywhere the stars and nebulae, magnificent in their cosmic grandeur, but to these things the Golden Amazon of Earth gave scant attention. The marvels of space were unimpressive by very reason of their familiarity. Her attention was concentrated on a small green world, a solitary emerald point in the hosts of the void, toward which the *Ultra* was sweeping with soundless and immeasurable velocity.

"It just can't be Earth," the Amazon insisted to herself. "So many light-centuries from its normal position—right in the Milky Way galaxy itself. Everything says it is, yet reason says it is not…and I prefer to trust my reason."

She relaxed again, puzzled, standing like a goddess with the stars for a backdrop. For once in her life, the Golden Amazon was bewildered. Her keen mind could not, as it normally did, hurdle the problem before her—and not without reason. How could a planet, the entire Earth itself, transfer its position from being one of a family of planets circling Sol to occupy a place of isolation light years of distance across space?

"It is a bit of a problem, isn't it?"

The Amazon turned sharply as the grave masculine voice broke in on her thoughts. Abna, her husband, had entered the control room—the seven-foot tall, majestic leader of the Cosmic Crusaders, as flawless in male attributes as was the Amazon in her sex.

Moving to the observation window, he looked on to space for a moment, then turned, quizzically smiling, to the violet-eyed, golden-haired woman beside him.

"Beyond all reason, isn't it?" he asked at length.

"Definitely!" The Amazon gestured toward the bench and its contents. "I've been checking over the details, and the maths arrived at by the main computer, but I can't find a mistake anywhere. Everything says that is Earth ahead—and the photos even show the planet's surface to be exactly identical to Earth, but I know at the back of my mind that it's crazy."

"Very strange," Abna agreed, shrugging. "We're in the middle of the Milky Way, and yet there's Earth only about two hours' flying time away, at the pace we're making. No use worrying, Vi; just leave it be until we get there. Then we'll soon find out."

"If only I had seen this, I'd think it an illusion," the Amazon said. "But you're seeing the same as I do—and so do Viona and Mexone. So it must be genuine…" She glanced about her. "Time those two were back on the job, isn't it?"

Abna shrugged. "They've fifteen minutes more yet. Let them have it, Vi: they don't get much chance to behave as husband and wife, remember. Always off on some mission, and it's usually us who are responsible. Maybe we ought to remember sometimes that they're only young—or rather that we're rather old."

"In comparison to them, yes," the Amazon agreed. "But not in any other sense."

Abna smiled and said nothing. The brief glimpse of the eternal feminine peeping through the Amazon's cold, scientific exterior had amused him. Though she had no reason to fear advancing age—for physically and mentally she was an apparent 25—she was still woman enough to reject any comment upon it. As for Viona, daughter of the Amazon and Abna, and Mexone, her husband, they constituted the remaining two members of the Cosmic Crusaders, the fabulous little band devoted to the self-appointed task of helping needy or backward people, on whatever planet, to a better position than they would otherwise have been able to achieve.

The present position for the Cosmic Crusaders was unique. At the close of strange experiences in the region of the Coal Sack, they had suddenly observed their own world some 80 million miles away. Now they were hurtling toward that world, each one of them intrigued, yet baffled. Reason and scientific fact were utterly opposed to one another.

The Amazon crossed to the observation window to join her husband. For a time they watched the emerald point growing larger, then presently Abna made an observation.

"Apparently Earth—if it is Earth—isn't the only planet in this part of space. Notice far beyond it again—there's another planet. Sort of pearl-gray light. It's plainly a planet and not a star. Presumably it has the same star for a sun that Earth has."

"Which is that G-type dwarf star some 80 million miles to the cosmic east," the Amazon said, pointing. "I've already had it under observation. At first I thought that by some fluke it was the sun of the Earth system, but I soon found it wasn't. For one thing it's slightly larger, and also a good deal younger, Similar to Earth's sun, but not identical… As for that pearly planet beyond, I never noticed it before."

Abna moved over to the telescope and adjusted the eyepiece. He peered long and earnestly through the lens, and then looked up and studied the self-registering instruments fitted to the telescope's side.

"Visually, there's nothing to report. Seems to be a

cloud-wrapped planet. Distance is some 40 million miles beyond Earth. General conditions seem about the same as Earth itself. That's as far as we can get—until we explore it ourselves."

The Amazon gave a worried smile. "We'll tackle Earth first; the rest can wait."

Abna rejoined her in window-gazing, then catching sight of the Amazon's definitely troubled expression, he put a great arm about her shoulders.

"Troubled, Vi?"

The Amazon and Abna glanced around as copper-haired, sapphire-eyed Viona came bouncing lithely into the control room, followed somewhat more ponder-ously by her husband Mexone. Viona hurried over to the window and gazed out into space, her brightly lovely young face full of eager interest.

"Old Earth still there, I see," she commented; then she looked at her mother questioningly. "It is Earth, I suppose? You haven't proved anything to the contrary in the meantime?"

"Nothing," the Amazon answered. "Science and common sense still don't agree, so as your father says, the only thing to do is go ahead and find out."

The *Ultra* still flew on with tremendous speed by reason of its constant velocity in free space, but pres-ently the forward jets came into operation, thrusting the huge vessel away from the approaching Earth and with this operation the speed began to noticeably slacken.

"There's no doubt that that's Earth—exactly as we

left it so many years ago," Viona said. "There's the United States of Europe—America, Canada, Africa, the Poles... And there are the British Isles, on the left of United Europe. Can't be any doubt about that."

"No use denying the evidence of our own eyes," the Amazon admitted. "Things being as they are, I think the best course is to head for the south coast of England, and my own home. It ought to be still standing as we left it."

With that she turned aside to the control panel again; and within twenty minutes the *Ultra* was sweeping through the outermost fringes of the atmosphere, going ever down. Yet the Amazon had none of the feelings of a traveler returning after long absence to her homeland. There was something different, something queer, and she couldn't put her finger on it. Earth in the midst of the Milky Way? No! There was something wrong.

Shaking her head to herself, the Amazon gave her entire concentration to the job of handling the *Ultra* as she leveled out over the sprawling mass of London. Taking the city as her landmark, she changed course gradually and headed southwards until the English Channel came into view; then she began the weaving back and forth which was necessary in order to pinpoint her own closed residence at the back of the South Downs.

By the time she had discovered the tiny white speck which was her home, the *Ultra* was moving slowly—not more than fifty miles an hour and at a height of about 3,000 feet, skimming over sun-washed fields and hedgerows, speeding over farms and small outlying towns—until at last she had her home directly below her, the grounds thereof expanding on all sides into park-like spaces. Slowly she lowered the immense vessel down, sweeping several times over the wide, grassy spaces, until at last the *Ultra* settled down to a vast green lawn, kept in perfect repair—and became still. The hum of the power plant ceased.

"And that is your home?" Mexone asked, staring across the lawn to the white, shuttered building not very far away.

"That's it," the Amazon confirmed, operating the controls that unfastened the airlock. "Though it must be many years since we left. Let's be moving."

Abna followed her, then Viona and Mexone. Mexone looked in wonder on the green grass and soft blue of the summer sky. He couldn't believe it, so utterly at variance was Earth with his home planet.

"Everything seems to have been attended to," the Amazon said, leading the way to the massive front door of the residence. "I left orders for everything to be kept in order until I returned, and that the house was to be examined and aired from time to time. From the look of things that has been done."

Gaining the front door, she spoke briefly. The lock, actuated electronically by her voice pattern and her visual image, opened and in another moment the portal was winging wide on to an expanse of exquisitely decorated hall, the furniture covered with dust sheets.

"Yes," the Amazon said slowly, entering and gazing

around her, "it's all the same as it ever was—even though I still don't understand it."

"It happened, anyhow," Viona said. "This is your home all right. I know it well enough."

Within an hour the four were more or less settled. The dust sheets had been removed; they had had a meal from provisions brought from the *Ultra*, and now they sat in the huge lounge, dressed as became normal civilians, not ashamed to admit they rather liked— temporarily at least—the respite from an incessant round of cosmic adventure.

"I'm not satisfied," the Amazon declared, tapping a long yellow index finger on the arm of her chair. "I'm perpetually overshadowed by the conviction that this is a dream or something. Outwardly, everything is as it should be—not a thing disturbed; but inwardly it just doesn't jell. How do the rest of you feel?"

"I feel the same as you do," Abna confessed, "but since we're in no danger or inconvenience, why bother about it?"

The Amazon, looked at him indignantly. "Why bother about it, did you say? We have to bother about it, Abna, because we know it isn't right. I shan't be satisfied until I know the answer."

"I'll wager this isn't Earth at all, but an illusion. I'm going down to the village store to find out."

Abna became silent. He knew of old the Amazon's peculiar insight. If she was convinced something was wrong, then invariably it was—but for the life of him Abna could not, at the moment anyway, see any clue to the mystery.

The provision store the Amazon had mentioned was in its normal position, a small driveway leading up to it. She opened the door, glanced up at the ancient-type bell clanging over her head, and then waited with Abna behind her for the proprietor to appear. He did so, after a moment—a tubby little man with sandy hair, just as the Amazon had always known him.

"Good afternoon," the Amazon greeted him, moving forward. "It's Mr. Pearson, isn't it?"

The tubby little man did not reply. He gazed over his counter blankly, then slowly scratched his head, a look of bewilderment on his face. The Amazon looked at him, frowned, then glanced at Abna. Immediately he took up the conversation.

"I know we've been away a long time, Mr. Pearson, but now we're back. Surely you remember me, Abna? And this is my wife, who was Violet Ray Brant before she was married to me at Westminster Abbey. Or does the name of the Golden Amazon mean more to you?"

The tubby man still did not speak. His vacant eyes went over the Amazon, as though he were absorbing every detail of her perfect, golden-hued figure in the colorful summer frock. The Amazon watched his scrutiny with one eyebrow raised and a faintly cynical smile on her mouth—but Abna went further and passed a hand quickly before Mr. Pearson's eyes. He did not even blink.

"Amazingly enough, he doesn't see us," Abna said, turning.

"Well, if he's gone blind—which I doubt from the sure way he came into the shop—he at least can't be deaf as well," the Amazon retorted. "Why on earth doesn't he answer?"

Far from answering, Pearson scratched his head and then sucked his teeth. He came shambling around the provision-littered counter, walked past the Amazon and Abna without seeing them, and then slammed the door they had left open behind them.

"Blasted kids," he muttered. "Always up to some tricks!"

With that he went back into the kitchen, leaving Abna and the Amazon staring blankly after him. Then abruptly the Amazon set her jaw and moved forward.

"I'll soon settle this—"

"No, wait." Abna gripped her arm and drew her back. "There's more to it than there appears. He didn't deliberately ignore us: he isn't blind or deaf, because the bell brought him into the shop. It's just that...we don't exist to him. He didn't even see us!"

The Amazon slowly relaxed as the truth of Abna's words sank into her mind. Presently she looked up at him quickly.

"Yes, I believe you're right—which bears out what I said about there being something queer. All right, we're going to look further into this, but first it might be a good idea to see from television exactly what's going on in the world."

"Fair enough, but there's no electricity at the house, remember. It may take a time to get it reconnected."

"We'll sling an extension from the *Ultra*'s power plant. Come on." The Amazon led the way swiftly to the door. Once again the bell clanged as she and Abna passed to the outside, but by the time Pearson had arrived to investigate, the door was shut again. What he thought about the whole business they had no idea; and in any case, they had other things on their minds.

They quickened their pace and before very long they had returned home. Preoccupied, they re-entered the lounge through the French windows. Immediately Viona and Mexone glanced up.

"Well, any news?" Viona asked eagerly, and the Amazon gave her a somber glance.

"News of sorts, yes—and decidedly baffling it is. We're just not visible to other people. We can create sounds but they're not able to see us, or hear our voices. By sounds, I mean we can ring the bell of a door, but when we talk we can't make ourselves heard."

The Amazon nodded toward the big television in the corner.

"That's the first thing that can help us. Should be easy to find a bulletin on one of the news channels so maybe we can learn something. We'll sling an extension cable from the *Ultra*'s power plant. Give me a hand, Abna."

He nodded and accompanied her outside. In less than ten minutes a live power wire had been carried across the lawn to the television set and switched on. Then the four of them waited, watching as the blank screen abruptly brightened and Amazon switched channels until the image of a news announcer came into view. The Amazon smiled in satisfaction and boosted the sound. The others tensed slightly as they concentrated on listening to what the news announcer had to say.

"…and as is customary at this time, this station is listing the accidents and crimes which have occurred within the metropolitan area during the last 24 hours. There have been over 460 fatal accidents, mostly in traffic; some 300 suicides, and 60 major crimes, in which murder has taken predominance, as usual. The matter of these accidents and crimes, which have been occurring daily now for nearly two years, is to be the main topic for debate at the forthcoming meeting of the world council. The world council has high hopes of solving why humanity should be so mysteriously hag-ridden… And now for the resumé of the news for those who may have missed the commencement of our program."

The Crusaders exchanged grim glances as the announcer paused before continuing:

"The Little Wars in Western America continue and there are signs of a further outbreak of violence in the European area. From London itself there is nothing unusual to report, beyond a further fall in share values on the stock exchange. From scientific circles comes news that it is hoped to presently institute a three-day-a-week service to all the colonized planets instead of two days as at present. The Dodd Space Line is considering this innovation at the moment. And finally, the reports on crime, death, and suicide, which are a feature of our present daily bulletins. And that is all the news from Universal television."

The Amazon switched off the television and considered for a moment, then she looked across at Abna.

"Something is definitely wrong," she said. "Apart from the Earth being out of its normal position in the cosmos, I mean. When we departed on our crusading journeys we left a peaceful, prosperous planet—otherwise we wouldn't have gone. Now it seems the planet is afflicted with war, death, crime, and suicide, to such an extent that daily bulletins are issued in regard to it. What's happened to change things so much?"

"I'm more interested in the fact that we're invisible," Abna said. "Yet for the life of me I can't see why we should be."

"Because—as I said before—I don't believe this is really Earth," the Amazon insisted. "It just looks like it—but suppose the people tenanting it are really millions of miles or even light-years away. They wouldn't contact us, would they?"

Abna frowned. "Just what are you getting at?"

"I am assuming—vaguely, I must admit—that this planet is somehow reflecting events on Earth, with such flawless perfection that we can't tell the difference, except in the way people react. Imagine reflections of people in a mirror. The reflections would not answer you if you spoke to them, would they? It's possible that scientists somewhere have perfected something far above that, even to the actual duplication of human beings, buildings, sounds, and everything else that goes to make up a world."

"They must have incredible science to do that," Abna muttered, still frowning doubtfully. "And anyhow, why do it? Where's the point of it?"

CHAPTER TWO
CAPTIVES OF THE DENAFRONE

It was just after midnight when they had finally retired. In the Amazon and Abna's bedroom the shades were undrawn, leaving the perplexing starry sky open to their vision. For a long time after Abna had dropped off to sleep the Amazon lay looking up at the hazy galaxies, trying to sort out in her mind what new puzzle had presented itself—but the more she thought about it the more baffled she became. And so finally she, too, fell asleep.

It was still dark when she awoke again—the soft, luminescent darkness of summer. For a moment she lay wondering what had roused her. In any case, she always slept on the edge of sleep, her intensely keen senses hardly subdued and ready for the alert on the slightest of provocations—usually dangerous ones.

Raising herself on her elbows, she looked about her, but could see nothing but the normal room.

Her gift for seeing in the dark enabled her to penetrate the deepest shadows, but there was nothing there. And beside her Abna still slumbered on... And yet, there was a something. The Amazon could feel it, even if she could not see it. It made her nerves tighten, and a conviction of electrical static set the short hairs at the base of her scalp tingling.

Then suddenly—a presence. At first it was only the hazy outline, then it rapidly gained density and formed into the general contour of a well-built, six-foot man in a dark tunic of some kind with a weird monogram inscribed on his broad chest.

"I believe," the presence said, "that I have the pleasure of addressing the Golden Amazon of Earth?"

It was a mellow voice. The words were well rounded and soft in their enunciation; yet behind them there was an infinite, disembodied coldness. There was no more human feeling in them than if they had been uttered by a robot.

"Yes. I am the Golden Amazon." The Amazon waited tensely. "To whom am I speaking?"

"To the First of the Denafrone."

"That conveys nothing to me, but I assume that by 'First' you are implying that you are the leading personality."

"Your assumption is correct, Golden Amazon. Maybe it would help things if you could see me more clearly."

The Amazon watched the tall figure stride across the room to the light switch. He seemed nonplussed as no light responded as he pressed the button.

"Dear me," he murmured; then after a brief hesitation he took something from his tunic and set it on the nearby dressing table. A switch clicked, and instantly the bedroom was flooded with pearly radiance. It was a strange light, soothing and yet intensely brilliant.

"Cold light," the First explained, as the Amazon looked puzzled for a moment. "The maximum of light with the minimum of heat."

The Amazon said nothing. She was studying the man's features. Most remarkable of all was his immense forehead, topped with glossy black hair. The eyes seemed to be gray and very sardonic beneath very thin, well-arched eyebrows. A fiercely hooked nose, thin-lipped mouth, and rat-trap jaw completed the definitely forbidding portrait.

"What do you want here?" It was Abna who asked the question, sitting up beside the Amazon and giving the First a grim stare.

"You," the First answered, shrugging. "Both of you—and the other two—Viona and Mexone."

"Why?" the Amazon snapped, not bothering to ask how the First knew so much, even to the intimacy of names.

"To myself and my race," the First said, examining his long-fingered hands thoughtfully, "you four represent a very disturbing influence in the heart of a great experiment. The disturbance-value is heightened by the fact that all four of you—and you two in particular— are extremely clever, possessing an impressive array of scientific weapons, including one which operates on the zero-quantity of thought. It is unfortunate that you happened to come into the midst of our experiments. You have only yourselves to blame for the predicament in which you now find yourselves. I have your space-ship under heavy guard. You may regard it as lost to you from now on."

Impatiently, Abna scrambled out of bed and dragged on a robe. As he tied the girdle about his waist he looked contemptuously at the First's sardonic face.

"If you will tell us what you wish us to do we can consider it. You will not find us uncooperative, and we're always ready to listen to another scientist."

"I am afraid this matter cannot be settled amicably, Abna. I repeat—you and your wife are interfering, unwittingly I know, with a profound experiment, and interference is something which can never be tolerated."

"You expect us, then, to depart from this world?" the Amazon asked, also getting out of bed and reaching for her wrap.

"More than that—much more. You will see later." The First reflected for a moment, then added: "I will allow you ten minutes to dress yourselves fittingly, then you will come with me."

The Amazon and Abna looked at each other. The First caught the glance that passed between them and added: "You will not make any attempts at escape because that would result in your being killed. This house is watched from every angle. Now, I will leave you to dress and pass on the same instructions to your daughter and her husband."

The First turned, but instead of heading for the door he went straight toward the wall, beyond which was

Viona and Mexone's bedroom. Mysteriously, he passed through the wall itself, and disappeared.

"Are we going to stand here and be dictated to?" the Amazon demanded, her violet eyes glinting.

"Yes—for the moment." Abna gave a shrug and pulled off his robe. "We seem to be in the toils of an educated and scientific gentleman who unfortunately has the whip-hand of us. Under such conditions it's wisest to obey."

The Amazon muttered something to herself and then became quiet. Silently she and Abna dressed, then together they looked out of the window on to the quiet of the grounds. The *Ultra* was still there, and as far as they could see, nobody was guarding it, unless they were inside it.

"Who do you suppose this creature really is?" the Amazon murmured. "What's he driving at?"

Abna did not have the chance to reply for at that moment the First was with them again. He stood for a moment by the wall, then surprisingly enough, Viona and Mexone, hastily dressed, came through it. They walked slowly, with an air of infinite bewilderment, as though they were not at all sure what they were doing.

"In case you are under the impression that these two young people have suddenly perfected the art of walking through matter, think again," the First said. "They did it because I made it so. The fourth dimension can be opened to others as well as to myself."

He came forward slowly, holding Viona and Mexone each by an arm.

"Mother, what's going on?" Viona burst out suddenly. "Who is this man? Suddenly he came upon us, ordered us to dress, and— Well, here we are."

The Amazon gave a grim glance. "You're as wise as your father and I about the set-up, Viona. As for this person, he's the First of the Denafrone. Apart from putting a guard over the *Ultra*, I don't know anything more about him."

"You will," the First announced, still with that ice-cold breath in his voice. "For the moment, all of you will come with me."

With that he strode to the outer wall and passed through it. The Amazon hesitated a moment, then went experimentally forward. To her surprise, she passed through the wall without effort and found herself standing in empty air some twenty feet from the ground, with literally no visible means of support. A short distance away the First was smiling coldly in the gray light of dawn.

"It is amusing to behold scientists of your high caliber mystified," he commented. "And remember, you only find the air solid and the walls as transparent as mist because I make it so. One false move and I could drop every one of you to the ground, with quite unpleasant consequences! Continue following!"

They went beyond the grounds to the open country beyond. Then it became obvious where the destination was. About half a mile distant, gleaming in the low rays of the rising sun, was a machine about half the size of the *Ultra*, and towards it the First was definitely heading.

"We've got to do something!" the Amazon said anxiously. "Once aboard that thing, and with our own *Ultra* left here, we've no means of fighting for ourselves." She laid a hand on Abna's arm. "Why don't we settle the issue now?"

"Here? In mid-air?" Abna looked at her doubtfully.

"Why not? It's only a drop of twenty feet or so when we fall. We've taken worse tumbles than that."

Before Abna could attempt any answer, the Amazon acted. She leaped forward and in two strides had reached the First's side. He turned in obvious surprise, and as he did so the Amazon's right arm lashed out with steel-spring impact. Her bunched knuckles struck him clean in the mouth and the force of the blow over-balanced him.

Evidently something else happened too. Probably his mind clouded for a moment. Whatever it was, the Amazon found herself dropping helplessly through space. She struck the ground violently and lay for a moment, stupefied. Then she became aware of Abna, Viona and Mexone likewise fallen, but slowly struggling to their feet. A little distance away, men similar to the First had appeared as if by magic and were watching the four narrowly, holding strangely designed weapons in their hands.

"I'm afraid that wasn't a very clever trick," Abna remarked, helping the Amazon to her feet. "And our friend doesn't look too pleased, either."

The First, who had also fallen, was being helped to

his feet by one of the attendant men. With subdued rage on his austere face, he came slowly forward. He wiped blood from his lips carefully.

"That," he said coldly, "was a senseless attack, Golden Amazon—the kind of thing I would have expected a low-type mind to do, but certainly not you. However, I shall not forget it, and it has got all of you precisely nowhere. Now get into that ship and don't try anything further!"

Grim-faced, the Amazon obeyed, rubbing her bruised shoulder as she moved ahead of Abna, Viona and Mexone, she entered a fairly large control room, but she had no opportunity to gaze around it. The attendants of the First, who seemed to be everywhere, seized her and forced her down a narrow passage into the metal stern of the ship. Here there was a metal-walled cell, just big enough to hold all four. They were bundled in, one after the other, then the metal door clanged shut and was noisily bolted.

"Now what do you suppose is going to happen?" came Viona's troubled voice out of the gloom.

"Nothing very pleasant, I'll wager," Abna said.

"Wonder if this place is ventilated?" Viona asked, dimly visible in the in the faint light reflecting under the metal door.

"Doesn't signify," the Amazon answered. "There's enough air coming under that door to keep us healthy. We shan't die that way. My main worry is having to leave the *Ultra*—"

She broke off suddenly and staggered against Abna.

He, too, lurched, and so did Viona and Mexone. A vast roaring broke upon their ears and enormous pressures weighed them down, increasing with every second, until it was as though they were pinned by a weight of countless tons.

Slowly they sank to their knees; then they were lying full length, fighting with everything that was in them to draw breath into their tortured lungs. For endless minutes the violent pressure endured until the four felt they could stand it no longer. Then suddenly it ceased, and with it the frightful roaring from somewhere beneath them. They rose slowly to their feet, aware of a sense of unnatural buoyancy.

"Evidently we're space-borne," the Amazon said grimly. "That must have been the take-off, and the noise was from the rocket exhausts somewhere beneath us. We've well and truly left our second Earth—and the *Ultra*—behind."

The others had no time to comment before the cell door opened and the First became visible, silhouetted against the lights of the control room at the farther end of the narrow corridor.

"I must express my regret at any inconvenience the take-off may have caused you," he remarked dryly. "If it caused you any severe physical discomfort, consider it recompense for the blow which you dealt me, Amazon."

The Amazon was silent, and though her fists were clenched in keeping with her emotions, she knew quite well there was nothing she could usefully do to alter the situation.

"You are wondering where we are heading?" the First continued. "I will tell you. To my home planet. You may have already seen it as a gray, pearly planet."

"We've seen it," the Amazon acknowledged briefly. "And when we get there, what do you intend doing?"

"I have many plans in mind," the First said reflectively. "My major concern is to be sure that you do not any longer interfere with our experiments. Apart from that, all four of you know many scientific things of which we are in ignorance. We intend to know what those things are. For the moment I will leave you. At regular intervals, food will be brought you, and you will have to make what arrangements you can for sleeping. None of these rigors would have come about if you had behaved yourselves."

The cell door clanged again and once more the four were in the faintly reflective gloom, each of them nursing considerable misgivings as to how the present situation was going to develop.

CHAPTER THREE
DEVIL'S WORKSHOP

The journey from the second Earth to the pearl-gray planet was not a long one at the velocity with which the space machine traveled; but for the four Crusaders it was definitely a prisoners' trip. They were duly given food, of sorts, and allowed exercise in the confines of the vessel under constant guard—but that was all.

So, still with no hint of what was in store for them, they came to the end of the journey—without the interest of seeing what kind of a planet they had come to. They could hear the rush of the atmospheric envelope against the ship as it descended, and the next thing they knew was that the constant throb of the power plant had ceased. Evidently they had arrived.

"We'd better be prepared for anything," the Amazon remarked. "And for about the first time in our lives we haven't a thing to defend ourselves with. Not a gun or weapon among the four of us."

"If we'd have had time to put on our flying suits instead of these ordinary clothes we'd have been better equipped," Mexone commented bitterly.

There was a sound at the cell door. A moment afterwards it opened and the First stood there.

"You can come out now," he said. "Go straight along this passage to the airlock. There you will join the guard who have full instructions as to what to do."

The Amazon looked about her. The ship had landed on a broad park-like space surrounded by curious-looking trees. Not far away several more spaceships were standing, and behind them again were quite normal-looking buildings, which, presumably, contained the executive offices, their bold fronts outlined against a sky of pearly vapors through which sunlight struggled fitfully.

"Quite a pleasant world," the Amazon confessed finally, evidently arriving at the conclusion that it would be better to be sociable to the enemy—for the moment. "What is its name?"

"Kolb. It is pretty similar in civilization to your own world, with the principal ruling city over there."

The First nodded to an endless mass of buildings, many of them skyscrapers, in the near foreground.

"The Denafrone are congregated there, and they constitute the government, of which I am the head. Otherwise, the people are engaged, in all parts of Kolb, on various pursuits, most of them having a scientific implication... But come, we have delayed enough."

The First made a brief signal, and at that the guards started to move. With the First bringing up in the background, the Crusaders marched about two miles to the city, entering it by way of two enormous opened gates, closely guarded. Thence up a series of very ordinary streets lined with immense buildings, and finally up the steps of one building in particular which, from its very massiveness, was plainly an administrative edifice.

Here the guards dispersed, but there were others along the great hall that led into the heart of the building. So eventually to a big, comfortably furnished room lined with vast windows, which looked out over the city. Here the journey ended. The First closed the room door and then came across, the thick carpet to survey the four as they stood waiting.

"Now, my friends, I can clarify the position," he said, eyeing them each in turn. "As I said earlier, each of you know, in various ways, far more than we do—scientifically. It is our intention to become possessed of that knowledge as far as possible. You know, for instance, the secrets of electronic contraction and expansion. You know, too, how to travel Time—"

"So, presumably, do you." the Amazon interrupted. "You have already given us a practical demonstration of your control over matter and the fourth dimension. There can t« little we can add to that."

"I am the best judge of how much information you can give! We want to know the secret of your method of Time travel. Also the secrets of electronic expansion and contraction; and above all, how your zero-quantity disintegrative apparatus works."

The Amazon smiled cynically, nothing more. The lips of the First tightened a little.

"My scientists are at work examining your *Ultra*, my friends. They have solved some of its secrets, but the others—those I have mentioned—have not been mastered. Therefore, you will supply the information I require."

"Supposing we did," Abna said. "What benefit would we derive?"

"Technically, none. You would simply have the advantage of meeting your deaths more comfortably than otherwise. Obviously, there can be no question of our sharing power. On Kolb such a thing can never happen. The Denafrone are supreme."

The quartet looked at him and said nothing, then as he motioned his hand, the guards went into action. Without ceremony they bundled the four out of the room and down the long hallway outside. They came to a stop presently before an immense grilled gate, which evidently gave access to an elevator.

Such indeed was the case. After a few moments, in response to one of the guards pressing a button, the elevator came into sight and the grilled gates slammed back. Once within the elevator itself the four began to wonder when its descent would end. It seemed to drop for an interminable time, and as it descended a growing heat made itself apparent, becoming a stifling humidity by the time the elevator finally halted.

Once more a grilled gate shot back and the four stood looking in silent amazement on the view. It looked like something out of Dante's Inferno in the few seconds they had to survey it before the guards thrust them forward.

In the near foreground were files of men and women,

practically Earthian as far as physique went, dressed in the most threadbare rags and hauling massive bars of metal on their shoulders. At times the burden was different in that it was a bucket containing a fluid of what looked to be molten lead. In other cases, masses of rock were being dragged by creatures who looked fit to drop.

Behind them in every direction were busily working machines, controlled again by emaciated, hopeless-looking workers. And behind all this was the intermittent flaring of enormous blast furnaces. These, combined with a drenching glare from overhead arc-lights, all contrived to set the temperature in the hundreds. The place was a veritable hell, a devil's workshop.

So much the four had time to grasp, then they were bundled forward again by the guards. They accepted the tough treatment meted out to them for the obvious reason that, at the moment, they could not retaliate. In this same mood of bitter silence they permitted themselves to be thrust and pushed across to an enormous brute of a fellow who was obviously the foreman, or supervisor, of this underground workshop.

What the guard said to him made no sense, but the outcome was plain enough. Without getting a chance to protest, the Amazon and Viona were seized by a couple of women guards and whirled away to a spot unknown. Abna and Mexone, for their part, were left in the foreman's care, and for a moment or two he surveyed them and then gave a slow, sadistic grin. Neither Abna nor

Mexone made any comment, but Abna for his own part weighed up the foreman carefully, noting his enormous stature—for he must have stood nearly Abna's own height of seven feet—and tremendous muscular development. A definitely dangerous adversary in any conflict that might arise.

Finally, the mutual appraisal over, the foreman jerked his head, and Abna and Mexone followed him to a low-roofed metal building stocked with a vast supply of uniforms. Two were whipped down from a shelf and thrown on the floor at Abna and Mexone's feet. The foreman did not say anything but his actions plainly indicated his meaning.

In consequence, Abna and Mexone quickly changed into the drab, chafing uniforms, and then followed the foreman outside again to the former spot. The Amazon and Viona were also there, likewise attired in blue uniforms. Shovels were handed to them and the guard indicated the furnaces and then the great hill of queer-looking fuel nearby. His actions said "Dig!" This much conveyed, he retreated to a short distance and stood watching.

"Nothing else for it," Abna sighed, easing his shovel into a comfortable position. "What all this business is about down here I haven't the least idea; but we're a part of it—whether we like it or not."

Dripping with perspiration, the four shoveled steadily; then there was a brief interval.

"The two things worrying me are the loss of the *Ultra* and the fact that we're not learning anything," the Amazon muttered. "We're just stuck her» as slaves and haven't learned a single thing. We've got to make a change somehow."

The others did not answer her. Again the furnaces opened and were fed. Again the relaxation—then suddenly Abna looked up sharply.

"Guards coming our way," he commented. "Wonder what we've done this time?"

In a matter of moments the guards had come up. As usual, they did not say anything, but their actions were to the point. They went straight to Viona, whipped away the shovel she was holding, and then gripped her arms tightly. Protesting violently, she was gradually forced away.

The furnaces opened and were fed. Again and again, endlessly, in the scorching hell. It was probably an hour later when Viona was returned to their midst by the guards. She was half carried into their area and then thrown down—and she remained down, unable to move.

"What the devil..." Abna flung down his shovel and strode over to her. As he gathered her up in his arms she stirred slightly and tried to smile—then across Abna's shoulders there came the lash of a fiendish five-tail whip, so violent be nearly dropped Viona out of his arms.

The lash came again, cutting deep—and it would certainly have descended yet again had not the Amazon intervened. Seeing what was happening, she threw down her shovel and vaulted forward at the precise moment the guard's arm was retracted for another downward sweep of the lash. Instead, the whip was torn from his hand and a pile-driver fist hit him clean in the face, smashing his nose and upper lip. He swung around in drunken surprise, to realize that the Amazon had vaulted on to his back and was clamping her right arm under his chin.

There was only one end to a hold like that, and the workers stopped their endeavors to watch. Slowly the Amazon's arm tightened as she strained her more-than-human muscles to the limit. The guard writhed and struggled. He fell on the floor and gasped for breath, feeling his head being forced farther and farther back with every second—until at last there was a pronounced crack. Only then did the Amazon let loose his dead body and go over to where Abna was still holding Viona in his arms.

"There's going to be trouble for that, Vi," he warned her. "Take a look behind you."

From then on things happened fast for the Amazon. With so many strong men about her, she was comparatively powerless, mightily though she struggled. She was forced across the workshop, watched by the workers, and ended up inside a cage-like affair like an animal trap. The door slammed and locked upon her and the guards retreated.

Straightening up, the Amazon looked about her. The cage was composed of inch-thick bars and there was very little room in it for her to move around. Naturally she could see in all directions, including the area where Abna and Mexone were being forced back to work. Viona was on the floor at the moment, but she got slowly to her feet as a whip lashed her shoulders.

Then, after a while, the Amazon caught sight of the First himself across the workroom. With his easy, dignified walk he came through the midst of workers and guards until he was outside the Amazon's cage. He stood regarding her, smiling slightly.

"Apparently, Amazon, you are in need of a lesson," he commented finally. "I have just been informed of your savage attack on one of my guards. I believe you killed him—broke his neck. While I have an admiration for your strength, it is obvious that such behavior cannot go unpunished."

The Amazon frowned, puzzling the matter out to herself. The First watched her reactions for a moment, then he signaled one of the guards and gave him brief instructions. What those instructions were became obvious as a crane with an extremely long extension arm came rumbling into view. From the arm a tough chain dropped a hook on top of the cage, then it was lifted into the air.

The Amazon held tightly to the bars as the cage swayed into space. The First looked up at her sardonically as the cage rose and was carried through a tunnel toward what looked like a volcanic fire.

Then suddenly the full awesome sight burst upon the Amazon's vision. The crane continued to the very edge of a steep precipice and there stopped dead, its extension arm, with the cage swaying on the end of it, jutting far out over a vast cauldron of molten metal. Perhaps it was natural, or perhaps a reservoir of molten metal. Whatever it was, it emanated the heat of Hades itself and dense sulphuric vapors rose from it in sickening clouds.

On three sides, and below through the floor bars, the Amazon could see nothing but the crater. On the fourth side the arm of the crane extended backwards into the comparative darkness of the tunnel. The Amazon was contemplating this solitary link with firm ground when she saw the driver of the crane emerging from his cab. Shielding his face from the heat, he tossed something toward her—something that unraveled as it shot through the air. It proved to be a small drum of wire, which hit the cage top and then dropped between the bars and at the Amazons feet.

Abruptly the cage jolted, dropped a dizzying six feet, and then came abruptly to a halt again. Flung to the barred floor, her heart thumping with the shock, the Amazon slowly got up again. The molten hell was six feet nearer. She looked up at the chain links. That slip had not been accidental. Something had actuated the winch mechanism causing the sudden drop—

Suddenly she grasped the First's sinister plan. The crane's winch was obviously fitted with delayed action-winch controls. At intervals they would operate, dropping the cage six feet lower every time, until the full thirty feet or so to the molten metal had been reached.

The cage dropped again at that moment, another six feet. The heat was crushing now and the smoke and fumes almost incessant The Amazon coughed for a moment, then twined her right arm in and out of the bars, so arranging it that her forearm—protected by the sleeve of the uniform she was wearing—was braced against one of the weaker bars. Again she paused, gathering all her strength, then she threw every ounce of her amazing muscular power into a steady, sustained effort.

Slowly, very slowly, the bar began to bend. Perspiration poured down the Amazon's face and veins stood out in corded knots on her forehead as she struggled. But definitely she was winning. The bar, despite its thickness, bent very gradually like a warm candle, until after three efforts the Amazon had forced it into a U.

Having got this far, she set to work on the neighboring bar, bending it in the opposite direction. When at last she withdrew her numbed, abrasioned arm and rubbed it fiercely, she had made an aperture just wide enough to permit of her slender body.

Down went the cage again with another sickening lurch. The fumes thickened to a positive fog, blinding and half choking her. One more lurch downwards and she estimated that the gases would finish her anyway... But she had no intention of waiting that long.

Quickly she squeezed herself between the bowed bars and then scrambled on to the top of the cage. To grasp the huge chain links was no effort and so, little by little, finger and toe, she climbed over the boiling caldron until she had reached the top of the chain and the comparative safety of the crane arm. Thereafter, clinging to the metal framework she found her way to the tunnel floor and looked about her.

Just as she did so, the crane driver came hurrying from the farther depths of the tunnel. Undoubtedly he must have been mystified by the Amazon's escape, but on the other hand he obviously did not know what kind of a woman he was dealing with or he would never have shown his face. Like many others before him the slender grace and apparent femininity of the Amazon fooled him utterly.

The Amazon waited for him to reach her, his hand gripping a weapon. He made a final lunge toward her, plainly aiming at seizing her—then he next moment he was flat on his face with the senses smashed out of him by a killing blow on the back of the neck.

While she thought out what she ought to do she climbed into the crane's driving cab, quickly figured out the controls, and then lowered the cage into the boiling maw. As she had expected, the molten metal liquefied the cage as though it were made of tallow— and obviously, had she been inside it her body would have gone, too. When she left the driving cab there was only the chain reaching down into the white-hot hell, and even that was severed where the links touched the metal.

Turning to the crane driver, she lifted him in one hand and dumped him back into the cab. Then she made a thorough job of tying him up with the various control wires, so thoroughly indeed it would take him a long time to extricate himself even when he recovered.

"In that time," the Amazon mused, surveying her finished work, "I hope I'll have done all I want to do."

Suddenly conscious of the passing time, she turned about and sped lithely up the tunnel along which the crane had traveled. She had no difficulty in finding her way: the crane had left a clearly visible tractor imprint. So, after perhaps ten minutes, she came back to the workroom, entering it from the farther side by means of an enormous archway. Cautiously she peered on the activity, weighing up the situation.

To her relief, Viona was still at work in the distance. She had evidently not been taken yet for her second 'session' with the First. Mexone and Abna were also there, continuing the dreary, back-breaking routine of loading the furnaces. But between them and the Amazon was a wilderness of workshop, watching guards, and danger with every step.

How to reach them? How perhaps to escape from the workshop and somehow get to the surface, situated some five hundred feet overhead? Safe for the moment, the Amazon dwelt on these problems, then her eye became attracted by a nearby intense brilliance. She glanced, and then looked away with dazzled eyes. An enormously hooded worker was at work with something like an acetylene welder, fusing two pieces of metal into each other. The stuff he was using was evidently something more potent than acetylene, otherwise he would have never have needed such elaborate protection. His suit was of the same design as that issued to a worker dabbling with atomic radiation.

He was comparatively alone: this was the thought on which the Amazon seized. The nearest workers were some yards away, all busy on their own tasks, and over this portion of the foundry-workshop there did not seem to be any intense supervision. The nearest guards, pacing back and forth, were quite one hundred feet away.

The Amazon made up her mind. She waited until the guards were pacing away from her, then she leaped forward quickly and grasped the astonished worker around the middle before he realized what was happening. Working at lightning speed, she dragged him quickly into the comparative protection of the archway and then pulled off his hood.

"Quiet!" she commanded, putting a finger to her lips. "You don't understand my language, I know, but you understand signals. Shut up if you know what's good for you."

The worker remained silent, whether he understood or not. The Amazon was working on the assumption that he was as anxious as she was to throw a spanner in the ruthless slavery exercised by the all-powerful Denafrone. He made no murmur as she signaled him to take off his protective suit. In the relative gloom of the tunnel, he watched her scramble into it and fit the welding cylinders over her shoulders.

Finally she put the hood in place, looked through the transparent face-visor, and signaled to the worker to sit down and keep quiet. He nodded and obeyed. Satisfied, the Amazon sorted out the details of the welding apparatus she carried on her back—then she stepped forward confidently into the workshop, so completely enveloped it was impossible to tell her identity.

CHAPTER FOUR

ESCAPE

The Amazon's first move was to return to the welding area. Here she appeared to be doing a welding job while she studied the next move. When her mind was made up, she waited for the guards to turn away from her, then she darted off into the midst of a crowd of workers where she would not easily be distinguishable. From here she worked her way toward the immense seven-foot supervisor as he stood with his back to her arrogantly surveying the industry about him.

Behind her face-visor the Amazon grinned, and it was not a grin of mirth, either. It was the grin of one who has the whip hand of a situation after adverse circumstances.

Poised, none of the workers paying particular attention to her, the Amazon brought the twin electrodes of her curious welding apparatus together and then depressed the operating switch. There was a sizzling flash of man-made lightning, unthinkably hot, which seared out toward the gigantic supervisor and caught him in the small of the back. He swung instantly with a scream of pain, and the searing brilliance struck him again, clean in the face. In that instant he dropped dead, his hair smoking horrifyingly.

That did it. The uproar that the Amazon had expected burst out immediately. Guards came flying from all directions, converging on their fallen boss. Workers surged, too, not fully aware of what had happened. In the midst of the stampede the Amazon made her way quickly through the surging throng to the spot where Abna, Viona and Mexone were standing watching the confusion.

"Vi!" Abna exclaimed, startled, as he recognized her face behind the visor mask.

"Out!" she shouted, her voice muffled by the hood. "We've got a chance to make a dash for it in this confusion, and I've got a weapon—of sorts."

She indicated the welding electrodes, and then she started moving through the confusion, pushing away workers when they hemmed her in, literally slogging a clear path as the others came up behind her.

The confusion was their greatest ally. Nobody knew but what the Amazon in her hooded outfit was an ordinary welding worker, for nobody except the dead supervisor had seen her activity with the apparatus. Abna, Viona and Mexone were, of course, obviously escaping prisoners, but with the guards all centered around the dead supervisor, and workers hemming them in on all sides, there was a comparatively clear stretch behind the workers toward the main doorway of the elevator, toward which the quartet were now heading with desperate speed.

Then suddenly they hit up against a snag. A mechanical truck conveyor loaded with ores, deserted by its driver as he joined the mob, came whirring straight toward the four from a farther point of the workshop. They made their preparations to dodge its drunken progress, and would undoubtedly have succeeded had not a young girl worker got in their way. Unaware of the truck, she came from the deeper reaches of the workshop to join the shouting crowd, and the truck was hurtling straight toward her.

The Amazon didn't ask questions, nor pause and wonder what to do. Though she and the others were now safely to one side of the truck, she knew quite well that the mass of metal and bogy wheels would cut the girl to pieces when it hit her.

The Amazon dived for the truck, her hands outflung. She hit it with all the force she could muster. It was the only move she could make, for there was not time to snatch the girl herself clear... For a breathless instant the truck heaved up on to two wheels; then under the force of the Amazon's impacting blow it overbalanced and crashed on its side, ores spewing and sharp-edged wheel whirring viciously. In one bound she grasped the girl, tossed her lightly on to her shoulder, and then streaked for the doors of the elevator where Abna, Viona and Mexone were already heading.

No word escaped the Amazon. She dumped the worker-girl on her feet and then slammed the elevator grille. A second afterwards she punched what she hoped was the right button on the elevator's side wall, and almost immediately it began to rise smoothly into the cavernous darkness of the shaft.

"Thank heaven for that," Abna muttered; then he stood watching as the Amazon rid herself of her clumsy protective suit.

"We're not out of the wood yet," she said quickly. "We've got to find some way out of this cage while we're still safe."

"But why, when it's taking us to the surface?" Viona demanded, her face troubled in the pale yellow of the roof light.

"Why? Because we'll simply ride from one captivity into another. You don't suppose the guards below will let us get away with this, do you? Either they'll stop the cage, or else they'll send word to the surface to nab us as we come up. We're going to defeat that possibility."

"How?" Mexone demanded bluntly.

"I don't know. We'll see…" The Amazon turned to the buttons on the wall and studied them. Finally she pressed one experimentally, and when nothing happened to the elevator's swift rising, she tried another button. This time there was an effect: the elevator slowed down and then stopped, the smooth black walls of the shaft visible beyond the gate grille.

"What now?" Abna asked. "We're not going to get far just poised between heaven and hell like this."

"We're going up the shaft," the Amazon said. "We know for certain that it leads to the upper world, and that's where we're going—but in climbing up instead of letting the elevator take us, we'll stand a better chance of escaping."

With that she turned to the welding equipment; then after a moment's thought she said:

"Turn your faces to the wall. I think there are dangerous emanations from this apparatus, but a short duration shouldn't cause any damage... I'm going to cut away the gate."

With that she scrambled once more into the protective suit and hood. Abna took the bewildered girl worker in his charge and turned her face to the wall. Then Viona and Mexone also turned away, watching their shadows brightly cut on the wall as the sizzling welder went to work. In all, the job only took the Amazon five minutes, then at a final kick, the remains of the gate went sailing outwards into the shaft. Seconds later there came the clang as it hit the bottom of the shaft.

"Okay," the Amazon said, wrenching off the protective suit. "I'll go first—and I'll take this equipment with me."

She strapped the welding equipment to her back and then eased herself out of the gateway. Clinging to its metalwork, she looked first down, then above.

"What about this youngster?" Abna asked, nodding to the worker. "She doesn't look as though she'll be capable of climbing."

"Carry her on your back," the Amazon answered briefly. "I want her with us. She may be able to tell us eventually what kind of a set-up really exists on this devilish planet.... Right," she finished, bracing herself, "follow me! Here I go."

She muscled herself up in the shattered gateway of the elevator and for a moment the others had a vision of her uniformed legs threshing wildly. Then they were drawn up out of sight and there was the sound of her on top of the elevator.

For her own part, her hopes were pinned on a bright star a seemingly infinite distance overhead. That, she knew, marked the limit of the shaft and the normal journey's end for the elevator. To reach it would be a long climb, but it had to be done.

So, typically, she commenced the ascent. She did it in the only way possible, by shinning gradually up the greasy cables from which the elevator depended. Now and again she slipped back, but on the whole she made steady progress.

One by one the others emerged from the elevator and started to follow her example, Abna having the hardest job of all with the girl worker clinging tightly to his broad shoulders. Somehow he managed the ascent, his giant strength just about equal to the task.

The absence of light was a drawback at first to all save the Amazon. She, with her gift for being able to see in the dark, made full use of the vague light reflected from the 'star' high above.

And it was as well she did, for presently her voice called down:

"There's a spot here where we can rest—let into the wall. Just follow my example."

The others paused, their legs scissored around the cables, trying to watch her movements in the dim light.

Vaguely they caught a vision of her swinging sideways until she leaped suddenly and clung to the wall of the shaft. After some effort, she succeeded in drawing herself up into a circular opening blacker than the rest of the shaft.

"Come up," called her voice. "I'll help you."

One by one the others obeyed, Abna coming first with the girl on his shoulders. With the Amazon to help him, he managed to successfully transfer himself and the girl worker from the cable to a large opening in the shaft side. After which it was a simple matter to help Viona and Mexone.

"Where are we?" Viona asked. "We're nowhere near the surface yet."

"In some kind of tunnel," the Amazon answered her. "Perhaps an inspection tunnel provided for the elevator shaft. If that is the case, it might perhaps come out on the surface somewhere... Anyway, we can rest for a moment."

Which was exactly what they did. They settled on the tunnel floor, backs against its wall, and gradually recovered from the labor of the climb they had made. Then at last Abna said:

"Presumably, Vi, you brought this girl along so she might help us. Do you want me to get busy on her and give her a knowledge of our language?"

"Hypnotically, you mean?" the Amazon asked.

"Yes; there's no better way without instruments. I can do it here since it's peaceful. Keep quiet while I have a try."

With that Abna turned to the girl seated quietly at his side. He could only vaguely descry that she was there, but she made no resistance as his powerful yet gentle hands caressed her face and turned it toward him. In some way she evidently sensed that he meant her no harm, but was trying to convey something of benefit.

So, in the dead quiet of the tunnel, he went to work, reading mesmerically into the girl's wholly receptive mind the entire basis and expression of the English language. For nearly thirty minutes he kept it up, then he gradually relaxed. Quietly his voice spoke out of the silence.

"Do you understand me? Have my mental efforts conveyed anything to you? Do you understand the language I am now speaking to you?"

"Yes, I understand," the girl said, her voice low and gentle. "I do not know..." She hesitated as she found words with a none too precise diction. "I do not know how you have accomplished this miracle of teaching me your language, but I am full of gratitude. And for saving my life in the work foundry," she added, leaning over Abna and addressing herself to the Amazon.

"I saw death coming straight at you," the Amazon answered. "The only logical action was to prevent it."

"What is your name?" Abna asked.

"I am called Silda. Silda Rafoon is my full name."

"We are Abna, Viona, Mexone and Violet Ray, my wife," Abna said, indicating each in turn in the dimness. "My wife is better known as the Golden Amazon. All four of us are from outer space and our sole task in life is to help those who are under domination and who are backward in scientific knowledge. We call ourselves the Cosmic Crusaders."

"I understand…" The girl's voice became wistful. "If it is your task to help those under domination, you could not have come to a world more needing it than this… Kolb is entirely dominated by the Denafrone."

"That is what we wanted to know," the Amazon said. "And other things as well. Who are the Denafrone, and what are they doing? For instance, what is the purpose of the foundry-workshop from which we and you have escaped?"

"It is but one of many under the leading city. None of us know what is really being done in the foundry, but all manner of things made of metal are created there and then transferred to the surface."

"Probably the same as steel foundries, atomic plants, and locomotive shops back on Earth," Abna suggested to the Amazon. "There things are run on a proper basis: here it is slave labor. I take it you are a slave?" he inquired of the girl.

"Yes. I, and my father and mother, and indeed all the population of Kolb are slaves. Born into slavery and dying in slavery. It has always been like that. The Denafrone of the upper world are supreme."

"What, precisely, is their ambition?" Abna questioned. "What, for instance, is their idea of a second Earth? Earth, by the way, is my wife's home planet, and there is a world quite close to this one, which is a duplicate of Earth. That was what attracted us in the first place, and we immediately fell foul of the Denafrone."

"So far as I can tell, the Denafrone want to find out what happens to a thinking race when its powers of thought are interfered with. Earth provides them with a whole planet full of people, of all ages and both sexes. Animals, birds, fish, and so forth are also included in the list. Simply, Earth is a planet like ours, containing people who resemble us and have the same thought-processes. Likewise, it has animals and so on, all of which are subject to this thought-interference."

"Mmm, I see," the Amazon said slowly. "But that still does not answer the question. Why do the Denafrone want to see the effect of thought-interference on a thinking race? Are they planning to overpower the Earth?"

"I do not think so. In any case, it is too far away to be in their sphere of interest. I understand there are other planets, comparatively near, which the Denafrone intend conquering—planets with beings like us. If the Earth-experiment is a success, then the same system will be used on the worlds that are yet to be overcome. That, I think, is the general intention."

"Plain enough," Abna said grimly. "They're making Earth a guinea-pig. If it works on Earth people, whom they regard as little better than laboratory specimens, then it will work on the populations of the planets they evidently intend mastering later on."

"Do you happen to know where the Denafrone keep their main laboratories, Silda?" Abna asked.

"Somewhere under their headquarters. That's all I can tell you."

"Somewhere under their headquarters," Abna repeated slowly. "And we came from their headquarters directly into this underworld. That suggests that while we're below, we might come across them. Even along this tunnel if we choose to go along it."

"We do choose," the Amazon decided. "Come on…"

"We've no light," Mexone cautioned.

"Then we'll try it in the dark. I can do fairly well in that direction, remember."

The only satisfactory thing about the whole set-up was that there were no signs of pursuit. As the Amazon had remarked, probably the Denafrone were waiting at the top of the elevator shaft for the fugitives to make their escape: it was unlikely they would ever suspect the tunnel.

Then just as they were congratulating themselves on their progress, something happened. There was a sudden jolt in the human chain they had formed. Silda screamed, and at the same moment there came the quake and rush of collapsing rock. Viona gave a shout of dismay as she suddenly lost her grip on Silda, and simultaneously the tunnel floor began to crumble beneath her feet. With a desperate effort she reached out into the darkness and more by luck than judgment clamped her fingers into firmer rock, Gasping, she slowly drew herself out of what she was sure was an abyss… Then the Amazon's welding apparatus flared in the darkness and in the effulgence the full disaster was evident.

Part of the tunnel floor had indeed given way after the Amazon had crossed it. She and Viona were on one side, and Abna and Mexone on the other. Between them was a gaping, crumbled blackness into which the luckless Silda had evidently fallen.

"I'm going after her," the Amazon said, shouldering the welding kit more comfortably, and with that she carefully scrambled over the edge of the hole, then felt her way downwards in pitchy darkness.

It was a nerve-racking descent, particularly as stone and rubble slipped with every move the Amazon made. But she struggled persistently, bracing herself ever and again on a firm piece of rock so she could operate the welder and have an idea where she was going. Thuswise she descended, and at a depth of about fifty feet felt something soft and yielding beneath her feet. A brief examination satisfied her that it was the outline of a girl's body.

Quickly, and risking everything, the Amazon jumped to one side over the obstacle. She landed safely. Evidently she had reached the bottom of the fault in the tunnel floor.

"Silda!" she exclaimed. "Can you hear me?"

"Yes—yes, I hear you." Silda's voice came out of the dark, speaking with obvious effort. "I—I'm here."

The Amazon moved toward the voice and then briefly operated the welding equipment. The evanescent flash of brilliance revealed the slave girl bent over a vicious spur of rock, which obviously had smashed against her back. She gasped hoarsely and moaned as the Amazon attempted to move her.

"Listen— Something I must tell you. Radio link…"

"Yes?" The Amazon waited tensely. "What about a radio link?"

"We have one. Closed circuit for—for workers only. Meant to tell you that. Might be useful to you—wavelength… four six two."

Silence again and then harsh breathing. With a thud Abna arrived at the bottom of the shaft and the Amazon felt around for his arm.

"Do something, Abna. She's dying. She just gave me a radio wavelength on closed circuit for workers only. I'd like to know more. Here she is."

The Amazon took Abna's hand and guided it to the girl's body. For a moment or two his fingers were motionless over her breast, then he gave a sigh.

"Too late, Vi. No heartbeats. She's gone, I'm afraid."

"Revive her if you can."

"No doubt that I can, but should I?" Abna asked quietly. "She's dead, and presumably passed to a happier existence than the slavery she's always known. Why bring her back to share the dangers that still face us?"

The Amazon sighed. "Yes, perhaps you're right. Probably I'm selfish: I just thought she could have helped us some more. All right, forget it. Leave her body where it is: it's a fitting tomb down here." She gave Abna a grim glance. "The Denafrone are evil. And have got to be stopped. Preferably by wiping out their entire planet."

"We can't do that, Vi." Abna shook his head. "If we did that, we'd also destroy Selda's people—those who've been enslaved by them through no fault of their own. Would you want that on your conscience?"

"No, but there might be a way…" the Amazon tightened her lips and gave a shrug. "Pointless to discuss it at the moment, though. Let's get on."

The advance began again, and it was mostly a fumbling progress, with brief flashes of illumination from the welder. The Amazon did not dare use the apparatus constantly for two reasons. For one thing, she had no idea how long the charges would last; and for another, she had no means of knowing if the emanations were really dangerous. So they had to manage as best they could, becoming thirstier and hungrier all the time.

"What's that?" Abna asked at length. "A star, or a shaft?"

The others stopped and gazed with him. There was something ahead, appearing to be slightly above them.

"What are we waiting for?" the Amazon demanded. "It's a light of some kind. Come on!"

They hurried their pace, yet withal took care they didn't accidentally land on any more weak rock. And as they progressed, the gray smudge resolved into a rectangular shape and so finally revealed itself as a heavy grating with light coming from beyond it. It was perhaps two feet above Abna's towering height as they came below it.

Interested, the four peered between the inter-lacings of metal, and beheld beyond banks of enormous generators, all humming to a soft whine of power. In another direction, as the four angled their faces, lay great panel switches. There were aisles and galleries, and all the paraphernalia of a great powerhouse. Particularly interesting in one direction was an obvious atomic reactor, of the type used on Earth for using nuclear power for peaceful purposes.

"Obviously a powerhouse," Abna said at last, glancing at the Amazon. "Maybe they use this grid for draining away waste."

"Or to create ventilation," she responded. "A strong current of ground air is usually demanded in an atomic powerhouse, and that is what this is. We—"

She stopped, nudging Abna quickly. He and the others looked intently towards a man on one of the galleries. He did not seem to be a slave worker. Though attired in working coveralls, his general bearing, as he studied and noted down the readings of various meters, was more of a man of science and considerable intelligence than that of a dispirited worker.

"There's a man who might be able to tell us something," the Amazon murmured. "If by any chance this powerhouse is connected with the thought-interference which is being hurled at Earth, then perhaps we can do something about it."

The Amazon tried the grating and it moved immediately but the engineer heard and came over to look down at them.

The Amazon sprang, her steel-strong fingers closing around the man's neck. With a terrific wrench she pulled downwards, with the result that the man came tumbling into the depths. He did not have a chance to recover himself. Flat on his back he lay gasping, the Amazon's fingers still on his neck, threatening him but not crushing him.

"What now?" Abna asked, moving forward, and the Amazon glanced at him in the light reflecting through the opening.

"It would be an advantage if we knew the language: we might learn a few things. What can you do about it while I've got him pinned?"

"Plenty. I can gather most of it from his mind. Here—let me take over."

The Amazon released her grip, and immediately Abna took her place, sitting astride the hapless engineer and gazing into his frightened eyes. At first ha tried to resist, then realizing Abna's strength was too great for him, he relaxed again and waited for what was to happen next.

Exerting his concentration to the full, Abna did not have much difficulty in reading the man's mind, chiefly because—not knowing what was happening— he made no effort to shield anything. Had he been of the same caliber as the First it would have been a different matter. Even as it was, there were one or two things Abna could not penetrate, but the details of the language proved simple. It was not a particularly difficult tongue in any case.

"Right," Abna said presently, in the Kolbian language. "Do you understand me?"

"I understand you," the engineer assented.

"Are you a slave worker, or a member of the Denafrone clique?"

"The Denafrone clique is supreme!" the engineer snapped, a gleam of resentment coming into his eyes. "Who are you that dares to challenge it? From your uniforms, I suppose you are escaped slave workers."

"Exactly," Abna acknowledged calmly. "And as such we are sworn to the overthrow of the Denafrone, and particularly the First... Now, answer some questions. How many others are in charge of this powerhouse?"

"None. I am supreme controller, and if I don't check the instruments quickly there may be trouble! This powerhouse is an integral part of the Great Experiment, and—"

"Oh, it is?" Abna smiled grimly. "Thanks for the information, my friend. Incidentally, what is your name?"

"Raol."

"Right. Now we are going up into this powerhouse you control and you are going to give me a lot more information. Our particular need at the moment is for food and drink, of which I believe you have an adequate supply. So your mind tells me, anyhow."

The engineer had no choice. He went to a nearby locker, unfastened the door, and brought out a large container, which, in special racks, had a variety of foods and drinks in tabloid form. Now he was in possession of the language, Abna ran his eye over the captions and decided which tabloids were likely to be most beneficial; then he turned to the others as they followed him up.

"We'll not take much harm with these," he said, indicating one variety in particular. "The make-up of these people is about the same as our own, so they must eat foods akin to ours."

The others nodded and started to eat and drink right away. This was no time, considering their hunger and thirst, to look a gift horse in the mouth.

Silent, Raol stood and watched, then presently he ventured a remark.

"I must look at my instruments. It is essential. Particularly the reading of the meters."

"Right—look," Abna agreed. "I'll eat as I come with you. I'm not trusting you out of my sight, my friend… And you'd better lock the doors in case anybody should interrupt us."

"Nobody will," Raol said, rather bitterly. "My spell of duty lasts till nightfall: only then will somebody come to relieve me."

"We're taking no chances. Let me see you lock them."

Silently, obviously not enjoying the orders he was being given, Raol obeyed. There were four doors in all to the powerhouse—enormous studded affairs of some kind of bronze-like metal—and Abna was not satisfied until he saw all of them shut. Deep in his mind he was wondering how he and the others had got away with it so far without recapture—and even now he had no guarantee but what some of the Denafrone were watching everything, and hearing it, by means of concealed television pick-ups. The only thing to do was take full advantage of the uninterrupted time.

Next, the engineer made a study of each of his meters. Abna tried, by reading the man's mind, to get some idea of what the vast set-up implied, but beyond the fact that the powerhouse used nuclear energy, he got no further. So finally, the meter study complete, Abna led the way back to the center of the powerhouse and looked at the engineer pensively.

"There is a lot of information you can impart to us, my friend. And if you value your life, you will do so."

"What do you wish to know?" Raol asked curtly.

"Many things. First, you have mentioned the Great Experiment. By that I assume you mean the experiments the Denafrone are making to the detriment of a very distant world, a world which is duplicated a few million miles from here?"

"That is correct," Raol assented. "I know nothing of the actual procedure itself. My job is to control this powerhouse, which makes the experiment possible."

Abna nodded. "I see. I rather wondered… Now, my friend, there is little more I can ask you: that lies with the Denafrone. But because you might give the alarm when we depart, it becomes necessary to do this—"

Raol waited, puzzled—then abruptly he remembered nothing more. Abna's massive fist crashed into the side of his jaw and flattened him unconscious to the floor.

"Rather distasteful, but necessary," Abna said, with a glance at the Amazon. "Better tie him up and gag him while we're about it. It'll delay reports about us."

No further time was wasted. A coil of spare wire was found and with it the engineer was securely bound. A waste-rag was thrust into his mouth and fastened there. No doubt the engineer would be found when the relief came to take over duty, but by then the quartet hoped to have accomplished many things. They passed into a corridor.

"Look out—danger!" Mexone said abruptly, moving backwards into the shelter of the huge doorway.

Even as they backed away the others saw what be meant. At the far end of the corridor, talking among themselves, were four of the Denafrone—and one of them, to judge from his attire and way of talking, was definitely the supercilious First himself. Luckily, they disappeared through a door.

CHAPTER FIVE
RELEVATIONS

Silently, alert for the first sign of trouble, the four moved along the corridor. There were doors to either side of them, adamantly closed, but nobody came from beyond them as they advanced. They were evidently in the private quarters of the Denafrone, regions situated far underground—perhaps for reasons of safety.

So they finally reached the main door. Abna placed his ear close to it while the Arnazon, Víona and Mexone took up sentry duty around him, particularly watching the right-angled corridor from which the Denafrone had originally emerged. For a while Abna remained motionless, then an irritated look crossed his face. He glanced toward the Amazon.

"I can't hear a thing. The door must be sound-proof."

The four moved together again and held a muted conference.

"Why don't we risk going in the room?" Viona demanded. "I know it's a risk—a terrific risk—but we're certainly not going to get anywhere by just standing here, and if we risk going down this right-angled corridor we'll sure enough run into a packet of trouble before long."

The Amazon and Abna were silent, thinking out the suggestion. Mexone gave a dubious glance.

"I don't mean charge inside in full view," Viona added. "We could perhaps glide in one by one and escape notice."

The Amazon came to a sudden decision. "All right, we'll risk it. You first, Abna."

"If the door's locked, we're no better off," he said, moving towards it.

There were no visible handles upon it so he gently pressed his weight against it. To his satisfaction it began to move slowly inwards. It seemed to be of immense thickness. Finally a long slit of light appeared and beyond it lay a vision of instruments. There came the low murmur of voices.

"I'm carrying on," Abna murmured. "I still can't hear them clearly and we may as well know what they're discussing."

He pushed the door wider and then silently inserted himself into a huge instrument room. It was not an actual laboratory as such: it had more the aspect of a precision-instrument department, with all manner of scientific gadgets and dials in various parts. Over everything was the customary shadowless white light.

Cautiously, the Amazon, Viona and Mexone followed up—then as Mexone, the last in the quartet, presented himself the door suddenly shut again, obviously actuated by a powerful spring. It made a distinct thud as it went back into position, enough noise indeed to alert the four Denafrone seated at a distant table. They glanced around and the quartet looked desperately around them for some place to conceal themselves.

There was no such place. The First of the Denafrone rose from his chair and came across, a weapon ready in his hand.

"Surprising, but not unexpected," he said. "Every part of the city has been advised to be on the watch for you after your escape from below... Kind of you indeed to come right into our headquarters."

The four said nothing, but the Amazon's hand slid gently to the controls of the welding equipment. Instantly the First saw her movement, slight though it was,

"I see no reason why you should be encumbered with that," he said calmly, and coming forward, he snapped open the buckles that held the equipment in place and then took it from her. Casually he threw it to a far corner of the laboratory.

"Evidently," the Amazon said bitterly, "we made a mistake in coming in here. At least we had comparative freedom before."

"Not for long would that happy state have existed," the First said regretfully. "In the end you would have been caught. It just so happens that you have been caught sooner than otherwise would have been the case... Now that you arc here, one or two things may as well be made clear."

"What things?" Abna asked curtly. "Or maybe you

are referring to the *Ultra*'s equipment?"

"It so happens that I am. I suppose your daughter Viona told you of my intention to learn the workings of the zero-quantity apparatus."

The four said nothing. They expected the First to take some kind of devastating action there and then— and they were prepared to go down fighting if he did. Instead, however, he gave a slow smile.

"Come to the point," Abna demanded.

"Wait a minute, Abna," the Amazon said quickly. "It's just possible that we may be able to make a deal with the enemy."

"What do you suggest?" the First asked, with a suspicious look.

"You say the only thing you require from us is the method of working the zero amplifier weapon. Very well: I am willing to tell you everything about it if you, in your turn, will tell us how you have made a second Earth."

"Very naive, Amazon. Why should I tell you anything when it cannot possibly be of the slightest use to you? Of what avail is information to those about to die?"

"Purely scientific curiosity, which rides over all dangers and even the certainty of approaching death; I'll be frank with you, First. We know the reason for your experiment with Earth—the real Earth, so far away, and we know you have duplicated the original to facilitate studying it. But we'd like to know how."

What was the Amazon aiming at, Abna wondered.

"So you know the details of our experiment?" the First asked slowly, controlling himself with difficulty. "You know far too much, all of you…" He stopped himself and thought for a moment. Then he seemed to come to a decision. "Very well, I will grant your request. Come over to this table. There I can sketch the designs which will explain things."

The four obeyed, Abna giving the Amazon a curious look as he caught her eyes. Naturally, she did not explain anything. She led the way across to the table and the three scientists seated, at it looked up stonily. The First gestured to them briefly.

"These gentlemen are mainly concerned with the Experiment," he explained. "I need not say more. Now, as to the information you desire…"

He murmured a few words of warning to his colleagues—which Abna fully interpreted for himself—and then he changed back to English and began his explanation.

"I am assuming, Amazon—and I think, correctly—that your scientific knowledge is of an order to grasp everything I am about to explain. First let us deal with space-time—the fabric of space. The scientists of Earth know it as a 'something' that transmits light, heat and other radiations, regarding it as an x-factor, which is to say they don't really know what it is, only what it does. But we of the Denafrone know that space-time itself travels in constantly pulsing waves throughout the universe, and we know that those waves can be directed. That is what we do."

"You have given me the basic facts of space-time as science knows it," the Amazon acknowledged. "Naturally, you have a good deal more to tell. How does the second Earth come to be?"

"It is not difficult to understand when you realize that everything transmits light, or a better word would be reflects. Everything, on any world, organic or inorganic, reflects the light that falls upon it and, therefore, it becomes visible. Those light-waves travel on into space forever and by instruments can be recaptured and reproduced."

"The light waves can, admittedly," the Amazon said. "But you reproduce the original object in exact form and size."

"Purely an extension of the basis of telescopic effects," the First said. "Imagine a neighbor planet to this one, very much like Earth in size and atmosphere, but otherwise an empty world which has never been tenanted by living beings. Such, originally, was the planet that became Earth 2. Let me digress for a moment to bring my point home— You are naturally aware how blank film, under the influence of developer, assumes a photograph of some object or other?"

"Naturally."

"Very well then. Imagine this neighbor planet treated with the special chemicals, which, as a photographic film resolves an image, resolves the light waves coming to it into exact duplicates of the original light waves. If that is a little hazy, try to see it this way. The neighbor planet is treated with resolving chemical, much of it composing the very materials from which an organic being is made up—lime, phosphates, water and so forth. On this world of ours here—Kolb—the minute light waves received from distant Earth are stepped up to their original size without any loss of definition and reflected back on to the neighbor world—still without loss of size or definition. The chemicals react to them and in the spot where the light waves fall a duplicate of the light-wave original takes form and apparent life, reflecting exactly what the original is doing."

"Quite ingenious," the Amazon said, after a moment's reflection. "In fact, a marvelous example of telescopic and vibratory power—for that is what it really is—raised to the nth degree. But what about sound? How is that reproduced? It only applies where there is air. Yet you reproduce it."

"But not the original sound," the First confessed. "The sounds heard on Earth 2 are there as a natural consequence of the duplicates doing the same thing on Earth. Naturally if a person say, rings a bell on Earth, that duplicate person rings a bell on the neighbor world as well, and the sound is identical. The same with speech. The original speaking, the duplicate does the same thing."

"And the time-factor?" the Amazon asked. "Despite the fact that light travels at 186,000 miles per second, it would mean untold centuries for light waves from Earth to reach here. That seems to suggest that everything on Earth 2 ought to be centuries behind—yet we know that is not so. It is definitely present day."

"Practically instantaneous," the First said. "The limiting speed of light does not apply in all cases, as you yourselves have proved. Light can move at any speed you wish it to if you apply the special physical means to *enhance* it. 186,000 miles per second velocity is only that of *unaided* light waves. We reproduce everything within seconds."

"I must confess to a profound admiration for your scientific skill," the Amazon shrugged. "What a pity it is wasted in such an unworthy cause... You duplicated Earth merely so that you could study the reactions of Earth-people at close quarters, after you had controlled their thoughts adversely."

"You are quite correct," the First answered coldly. "I would remark, however, that we do not consider the cause unworthy. There is a very definite reason for what we are doing."

"So we understand," Abna commented shortly. "The mastery of other worlds near this one by the simple process of mental control. But you had to have guinea pigs first... We know all the facts."

The First seemed once again to control an impulse to anger. When he spoke once more his voice was as smooth as ever.

"Our experiment is our own concern, my friend, and there is nothing you can ever do about it. As for the thought control itself, it is comparatively simple. Merely the transmission of amplified thought across space..." The First paused for a moment, then on one of the many draft sheets on the table he drew an intricate design, complete with all the scientific details. Finally he looked at the Amazon. "There it is, Amazon—the method by which everything is done, as I have already explained it to you."

The Amazon nodded slowly. Then she said:

"I assume that your hold over Earthlings is powerful enough to stop any of them thinking for themselves?"

"Entirely so. Would it matter if it were otherwise?"

"It might. You have deliberately forced a channel through space to carry your transmissions. If anybody at the other end were clever enough to reverse the process, the 'rebound' might cause considerable damage here on this world. Similar to throwing a rubber ball with terrific force against a hard wall. The effect of recoiling space, which you have apparently stretched to the limit of safety according to these figures, would be cataclysmic. And the reaction would come exactly back to the source by reason of space being strained from one particular place... You understand?"

The First shrugged. "A needless theory, Amazon. Nobody on Earth knows what we are doing, where we are, or has free will enough to cause trouble. Scientifically, what you say is correct, but we have no need to worry over it." There was silence for a moment, then the First added: "Well, I have kept my promise to you, Amazon, and given you every detail, have indeed betrayed far more than I intended. I ask you now to describe the zero-quantity machine and its workings."

"Certainly. The operation of the machine is simplicity itself. You have discovered already that it amplifies thought?"

"Certainly—on the same lines as our own thought amplifiers."

"Very well then. Everything being material in construction, that very material aspect is subservient to the higher quality of pure thought. That means that the power of a single thought raised to zero is the greatest destroyer in the Universe, for the simple reason that it cancels out all material things—or rather whatever material thing is concentrated upon."

The First's eyebrows rose. "Of course! Such a simple fundamental fact. The absolute of nothingness must be annihilation since the material is always mastered by the mental. The fact that you have not told me a lie is obvious from the self-evident formula you have given me. Surprising we never thought of that."

"The greatest of scientists balk at the simplest of problems," the Amazon added; then she avoided the critical eyes of Abna as he turned to her. He had never expected her to give the valuable formula of the zero-quantity machine, and for the life of him he could not understand why she had done so.

"We have, exchanged much information," the First said, with a sudden concession to pleasantry. "Before you die, Amazon, you may be interested in our final moves. First, we have no longer any use for the duplicate Earth: we have learned all we need to know as regards mental control over physical beings similar to ourselves. That being so, the illusions of Earth 2 can be destroyed."

"But will not doing that cause Earth creations to be destroyed, too?" the Amazon asked, thinking.

"No. The cause of duplication will be cut off from Earth, and therefore it will not be affected. If we could destroy Earth and its creations that easily we would do so." With a grim smile, the First turned and from the table picked up an instrument similar to a telephone. He spoke briefly in his own language.

"Cut out generators seven and two. Neutralize formula 10."

He replaced the phone and added: "In an hour the creations of the duplicate Earth will cease to be. But for Earth itself there is a final mental command, in which I think you will be interested."

He moved to a radio and livened the microphone. Once again he spoke, in his own language.

"Release final order... That is all."

He switched the radio off again and turned to the Amazon, a gleam of cold triumph in his eyes.

"I feel I owe it you, Amazon, to explain what I have done. I have given the order for the final command to be issued to Earth people. As you are apparently aware, the thoughts that have been conveyed to them have led them to seek a line of murder, suicide and destruction. The ultimate order is for the destruction of the planet itself, mainly because we have no further use for it. We believe that order will be obeyed. It would have been given soon in any case, but I see no reason why you—of Earth—should not enjoy the transmission of that order."

"What is the order?" the Amazon asked, her voice giving no indication of the inner fury she was experiencing.

"Your scientists, at the four corners of the Earth, will place magna-bombs in secret places, such places as will cause the ultimate of stress on the planet when they explode—as they surely will. It will be done under the guise of each one preparing a means of defense against the other. The subtlety of the plan comes in the fact that all bombs in the four corners of the planet will explode simultaneously. The outcome of that will be the total annihilation of Earth. Which is as it should be, since we have no longer any use for it, and when our influence is removed and turned on other worlds, we don't want Earthlings to start remembering the things they have done, and perhaps inquire further."

The Amazon said nothing as she assessed the situation. Magna-bombs, as she well knew, were the most violent bombs known to science—super-products of the one-time hydrogen bomb. Even four of them exploding simultaneously could produce a catastrophe, and if the First was to be believed, there would be far more than four.

"How long," the Amazon asked quietly, before the bombs explode?"

"Probably two of your weeks. Yes," the First reflected, "it will take that long for your scientists to place the bombs, and issue the necessary propaganda concerning them. Have no fear but what they do it: as long as our thought waves hold them, as hold them they will, they will obey implicitly."

"I take it the thought waves are not yours or your colleagues," the Amazon remarked. "Otherwise why are you here?"

"The thought waves were recorded a long time ago by picked members of the Denafrone, and are even now being transmitted—as all the others have been—by the spatial powerhouses."

The Amazon nodded slowly, apparently thinking. Then suddenly, so fast nobody saw it, her right fist lashed out with devastating force straight into the First's sardonically smiling face. Behind the overwhelming blow was all the force of the Amazon's astounding strength, plus her rage at the way Viona had been treated at the hands of the Denafrone generally.

The First literally shot backwards over the table his head twisted backwards on his neck. He crashed into the midst of the two men on the other side of the table, bowling them out of their chairs to the floor. The remaining man leaped up in alarm, then flattened to the floor as Abna's bunched knuckles smote him a shattering blow on the back of the neck.

"Finish them!" the Amazon ordered, her eyes bright. "It's our only chance. I'll explain later. Wipe them out, for the intellectual vermin they are!"

She leaped to continue the attack even as she was speaking, her main objective being the First—until a quick examination satisfied her that the blow she had delivered had broken his neck. On that she turned, hurling herself on the fourth man, who was just struggling from the floor. In her merciless hands he stood no chance, any more than the other two men in the hands of Abna and Mexone. Viona, for her part, stood on the fringe of the brief fracas, her eyes darting toward the door.

Within three minutes it was all over. Four of the highest officials of the Denafrone had ceased to be. Breathing hard, the Amazon looked down on them, a gleam of satisfaction in her purple eyes

"Where does this get us?" Abna demanded. "I agree they needed exterminating, but then there are a lot more of them all over the city. The Denafrone is no small, footling organization."

"There are four of them and four of us," the Amazon said. "That was the fact which registered with me. We are going to take on their identities and you, knowing the language, are somehow going to get us through the toughest parts. There's no time to lose. We need their uniforms. Come on—get busy."

No further time was wasted. The four Denafrone chiefs were stripped of their outer uniforms and, with some difficulty, the quartet put them on over their workers' garb. Abna had the greatest difficulty, owing to his great size, but by removing his working tunic and forcing himself into the uniform worn by the First—the tallest of the Denafrone—he did succeed in making the outfit fit, even if it was extremely tight in places. Fortunately it was made of a stretchable material.

"Are there women in the Denafrone clique?" Abna asked. "If not, it won't be easy to explain you and Viona away."

"We'll risk it. We've got many things to do. The first is to get a spaceship as fast as possible and fly to the neighbor world, and the *Ultra*. Once we've got the *Ultra* back, we can do many things."

"Such as?"

"We've got to get to Earth and stop that magna-bomb technique," the Amazon replied. "If we don't, Earth itself will be annihilated. There are two weeks roughly in which to cover several light centuries. It's the only way. We can never crack up the defenses on this planet, anyhow... Let's move."

CHAPTER SIX
RETURN TO EARTH

In a few minutes the four had left the instrument room, a task that presented no difficulty since there was nothing particularly complicated about the door lock. They left the half-clothed members of the Denafrone exactly where they were on the floor, and then proceeded up the right-angled passage outside. They were alert for every move, yet on the other hand they did not move with any furtiveness. They moved exactly as became members of the ruling race.

"Now for some fun!" Abna murmured, his eyes narrowing. "This is where we run the gauntlet, with a vengeance."

"Don't you realize where we are?" Viona asked. "This is the same hall we were brought into before the First packed us off underground. We've returned to it by a sort of 'backstairs' route."

"She's right—" the Amazon started to say; then she paused as she gave a quick glance at the corridor windows. "It's night outside," she whispered. "Maybe that will help us."

"Once we get outside," Abna responded. "We've got these guards to convince first… Leave the talking to me."

He strode forward, the other three behind him. In a moment or two they came to the first guard and Abna breathed an unnoticed sigh of relief. There was no chance of the guard recognizing the fugitives. He was not one of the men who had been on duty earlier. Evidently the guard had been changed in the meantime. Just the same, an expression of faint suspicion crossed his face as his eyes surveyed the four. Before giving him a chance to come to any conclusion, Abna stopped and faced him.

"Well?" he demanded, in the Kolbian language. "Why such an expression?"

"I humbly beg your excellency's pardon," the guard muttered. "It is just that your faces are not familiar to me, and therefore I was—"

"How dare you?" Abna barked. "Must the supreme Denafrone make himself known, in all its members, to the mere guard? Remember your place in future or the First shall hear of it!"

"Yes, Excellency. I am sorry, Excellency."

Abna turned to move on, then he stopped again. He thought for a moment and asked a question:

"Which of you guards is in charge? There must be a leader among you."

"I am the leader, Excellency."

"You are? Good! Dismiss the rest of the guard from this hall at once."

"But, Excellency, without the First's express wishes—"

"Enough! I speak for the First. Let us have no more insolence. There is a reason for my request. A matter of privacy."

Entirely unsure of himself, but evidently afraid that he might risk the First's displeasure if he did not obey, the guard raised his voice in a brief command. Instantly the remaining sentries on duty marched into the center of the corridor, turned like clockwork, then went 'left-right' to the darkness of the interior, and disappeared. The Amazon, Viona, and Mexone watched this performance with silent interest, and wondered vaguely what kind of pressure Abna had brought to bear.

"Now," Abna resumed, turning back to the guard, "as Captain of the Guard you are entitled to an explanation. All I can tell you is that we have been in conference with the First and he has told us of four slaves who have escaped this planet."

"Escaped?" the guard repeated. "I have no knowledge of that."

"That is not surprising. The Denafrone is hardly willing to admit that four slaves have escaped from under its nose. However, it seems that they have been recaptured in outer space, a million miles from Kolb, by alert members of the Denafrone space defenses. They are awaiting questioning by those who understand their language. That is why we are here."

Something of a struggle seemed to pass over the guard's face as he endeavored to make sense of Abna's bewildering story. He seized finally on what seemed to him to be a solid fact.

"Then you members of the Language Section of the Denafrone, are here specially to deal with the fugitives? That may account for my not having seen you before."

"Possibly," Abna agreed, with the brevity of officialdom. "I thought it best to explain to you, as Captain, without the rest of the guards hearing. The Denafrone does not like to admit mistakes. Quickly, now—we must be on our way. You can save our time by directing us to the space grounds in the quickest route. We are not familiar with this part of Kolb."

"Do you wish, Excellency, that I should conduct you to the space grounds?" he asked.

Abna looked into the street beyond. Overhead was starry darkness but the street was relieved into brightness by the usual method of concealed and shadowless lighting. He recognized the environment from earlier experience—and the distant gates heavily guarded. Beyond them, he remembered, were the space grounds on which the First's vessel had landed on arrival from the duplicate Earth.

"You had better come with us," Abna decided at length. "It is possible that the gate guards, not being familiar with us, may make difficulties and thereby cause further delays. You can deal with them instantly as captain of the guard."

For perhaps five minutes the advance continued, then at a sudden buzzing from his wrist the guard stopped and raised his right arm. He pulled back the heavy cuff of his tunic and revealed an object not unlike a wristwatch. Upon it was a lever that he quickly depressed. A voice, faint and yet clear, came forth from the tiny radio receiver. As was to be expected the voice was speaking in the Kolbian language. Intently Abna and the guard listened to it.

"Alerting all guards! Be on the watch for four fugitives wearing the uniform of the Denafrone, two women and two men—one man exceptionally tall. These four have murdered the First and his immediate advisers, and the warning call is—"

Abna did not wait for any more. He swung up his right fist with smashing power, and knocked the guard clean out. Then he turned swiftly.

"Run for it!" he said quickly. "They're on to us! They've found the First. But we might just make it to a spaceship."

"We've got to," the Amazon said grimly, bursting into a run. "It's our only chance!"

With the speed of track runners they all streaked towards the distant space grounds, aware that behind them in the city there was the wailing of an alarm siren. Obviously somebody had found the chief officials of the Denafrone had been killed, and the heat was on with a vengeance. Probably, too, the gate guard had added his own suspicions.

The space grounds came nearer as the four ran on. They could see signs of men moving back and forth between the huge array of spaceships, probably guards on the watch.

"Have to smash our way through somehow," the Amazon panted. "Without weapons there's nothing else we can do."

Abna nodded, speeding along. "We'll take the first ship we come to and chance it. You hear that, you others?"

"Right!" Viona and Mexone agreed together.

As they neared the space grounds, they lashed out at the guards, who were confused by their uniforms.

Four of the guards stumbled backwards and fell over, two of the others were tripped up; the rest yanked out their guns. By this time the four had passed, streaking with terrific speed to the nearest spaceship. Savage, crackling jets of fire followed them, missed, and gouged pieces out of the spaceship towards which they were heading.

Abna stumbled through the airlock and the Amazon followed him. Mexone came next—then Viona gave a gasp as a searing slash of fire carved her right shoulder. She swayed and would have fallen had not Mexone grabbed her. Without ceremony he bundled her, half fainting, into a small control room and the Amazon slammed the airlock

"Done it!" she exclaimed, swinging around. "Get going, Abna—quickly!"

He did not need to be told. While the Amazon snapped on the ceiling lights he took a look at the unfamiliar control board.

"Have to guess at it," he said shortly. "Here goes!"

He seized hold of an important-looking red lever and yanked it downwards. Immediately there was the buzzing of a power-plant from somewhere in the middle of the snip. At the same time the glass on the outlook port zig-zagged into a tracery of fine lines as fire from one of the guards' guns hit it.

Abna glanced, and nothing more. He read the notes in the Kolbian language above the switchboard, selected what he took to be the starting button, and pressed it... The result was immediate. The vessel started to rise, with terrific speed, blasting a fire of exhaust behind it. Obviously such tremendous accelerative take-off was not the normal thing and it flung the quartet on the floor and held them there, their ears deafened by the high-pitched scream of the machine's passage through the atmosphere of Kolb. This died away within seconds, and gradually weightlessness made itself felt as Abna struggled forward and pressed first one button and then another, until at last he had just enough accelerative power to provide a semblance of normal gravity. Only then did he get up from the floor and help the others to rise.

By now, Kolb was of no more than tennis-ball size in the hazy background of the Milky Way, while Earth 2 on the other hand loomed enormous and gray, its atmosphere torn into a tumult of hurrying vapors by some huge disturbance going on underneath them. What this something was they found out quickly enough when the space machine finally plunged below the cloud layer. The view was of twilight quality, hazy and unreal—and it was one of utter chaos.

Gone were the creations of Earth in mellow sunlight. Instead the sun filtered through angry, scudding clouds upon a landscape that had mysteriously become like treacle. Everywhere it was flowing and reforming, an incredible ocean of dissolving substances that was somehow revolting. There did not seem to be any solid land anywhere.

"So this is what happens when the duplicating influence is removed!" the Amazon said grimly, staring down. "Everything is in a state of flux. Where the *Ultra* is in this mess heaven only knows."

* * * *

An hour passed; then two hours. Abna gave a grim look from the control board. Then abruptly Viona—her shoulder injury having been healed by Abna—caught the Amazon's arm and pointed excitedly through the damaged window.

"The *Ultra*! Look!"

Just for a second the Amazon looked downwards, then as quickly looked up. Ahead of them, climbing to the heights, was the unmistakable shape of the great spaceship. At the same moment Abna saw it too and his mouth opened in amazement.

"Why didn't we think of that?" the Amazon snapped. "The First said they had learned all about it—which means they know how to control it. Only the zero-quantity machine defied their efforts. They've escaped from this morass, for which we can hardly blame them."

Abna was scarcely listening. He snapped controls on the switchboard and darted after the *Ultra* as rapidly as he could go. In the space of five minutes he had completed the journey through the atmosphere and was out in space, staring through narrowed eyes at the *Ultra*, floating majestically a little distance ahead.

"What now?" he demanded. "They don't seem to have seen us, or they'd let us have it with the weapons there are aboard..."

"Why?" the Amazon asked pointedly. "They don't know we're inside this vessel, and they know it is a Kolbian machine. Maybe they think it's Denafrone inside here— That's the angle," she finished urgently. "The only way to get aboard. You know the language, Abna. Radio to them and spin them a yam. We may be able to fool them."

Abna dived for the radio equipment and the Amazon took over the controls. Snatching the microphone to him Abna began to intone.

"Calling Earth ship. Calling Earth ship. The Denafrone speaks!"

After a moment or two the loudspeaker came into action and a voice responded in the Kolbian language.

"This is Exeber Jant speaking, leading investigative scientist. Who calls?"

"The First," Abna answered impressively, in a very good imitation of the First's voice. "I am here to determine what happened to the Earth ship when the duplicating influence was inadvertently removed. Do I understand you are quite safe?"

"Quite safe, Excellent One. We escaped without harm in the general chaos. The Earthlings have created a marvelous vessel… Your immediate orders, Excellent One?"

"I am coming aboard—"

Abna looked through the window and gave a start. Four machines of the Kolbian space fleet were approaching, and at no great distance, either.

"You were saying, Excellent One?" prompted the voice over the speaker.

"Er—yes. I am sorry: I was musing upon something. I have decided to come aboard. Frankly I am rather puzzled at the moment. You will observe four other space machines approaching?"

"Yes, Excellent One. Are they not part of your entourage?"

"Three of them certainly are, but the fourth one—a little behind the others— puzzles me. I am wondering if, perhaps, it might contain the four Earth people who have been trying to make an escape into space… Take heed, Jant! If you get a radio communication contrary to my orders it must be ignored. It may be a trick, to recapture the *Ultra*."

"I understand, Excellent One. What are your orders at the moment?"

"Place airlock to airlock," Abna said, his eyes on the approaching fleet. "I will attend to the rest. Hurry!"

"At once, Excellent One."

Abna switched off and explained briefly to the

others. When he had finished the Amazon smiled triumphantly.

"Classic example of turning the tables," she said. "But what's going to happen when you get aboard the *Ultra*? They'll know in a moment you're not the First. Your very size gives it away."

"Leave it to me. I'll think of something primitive, just as long as I get aboard."

Abna took the controls of the machine and jockeyed it into position, until presently there was the dull bump occasioned by the two vessels coming together.

Immediately airlocks were opened, and the enormous suction between the two orifices made the small ship and the giant *Ultra* all one as far as atmospheric pressure was concerned.

"Here I go," Abna said, giving the Amazon's shoulder a brief and encouraging clasp.

He darted with lithe movements through the airlocks and was at once in the narrow metal passageway that opened out into the *Ultra*'s control room beyond. Intently, the Amazon, Viona, and Mexone watched what happened. They could not see much since the Denafrone in charge of the *Ultra* were just round the corner of the wall, presumably near the switchboard and observation window.

Abna proceeded to the end of the corridor, then paused, cautiously peering into the control room. He felt sure of himself because he was on familiar ground. His eyes settled immediately on four men of the Denafrone, obviously the four scientists who were engaged on the investigation of the *Ultra*.

So much Abna took in; then he acted. Even as the men turned at the sound of his movement he was upon them. They were not quick enough to grasp the situation. Expecting the First, this seven-foot giant with the blond hair was completely outside their reckoning—and so was his strength. Two of the men he knocked out instantly with pile-driver blows. The other two men gathered their wits together and tried to hold him—but he was too quick for them. Instantly his mighty arms were about their necks and their heads crashed together with blinding force. The senses hammered out of them they sank weakly to the floor.

"Come on!" Abna yelled, looking down the corridor into the control room of the Kolbian vessel. "The coast's clear. Get these men into the other machine."

He lifted two of them, one in each hand, as he spoke and carried them down the narrow corridor. The Amazon and Viona, with Mexone helping, brought the other two. Finally all four were dumped like so many dummies on the floor of the Kolbian machine. Then Abna set the airlock time switch and hurried back into the *Ultra*.

"They'll just drift until they recover," he said, as the Amazon glanced at him. "Or until our pursuing friends decide to investigate on their behalf."

The others did not respond. They listened for, and presently heard, the deep squeegeeing noise as the Kolbian machine's airlock closed. Instantly Abna shut the *Ultra*'s own airlock by depressing the switch; then he darted over to the observation window and saw the Kolbian fleet in pursuit.

He jerked the power lever into the second and then third notches, which resulted in the *Ultra* taking a tremendous dive forward, so much so it pressed the Amazon tightly back in her seat and Viona and Mexone clung to each other under the force of the acceleration. Abna held onto the switchboard tightly, watching through the window as the Kolbian fleet, and the looming world of Earth 2, literally fell away into the gulf. Within five minutes the Kolbian fleet had been lost to sight.

"Good!" Abna said finally. "They can never keep up with us, anyhow."

He cut the speed down again to normal, then crossed over to the Amazon.

"Let's get our plan of action straight, Vi," he said seriously. "We're returning to Earth. That it?"

"That's it," she assented. "As fast as we can possibly go."

"We've many light-centuries to cross to get to Earth, and only two weeks before disaster strikes the planet. The only thing we can do is pass aside into hyperspace on the way and foreshorten both Time and space. That way we can telescope the light-centuries by using the fourth dimension."

"We'll do that," the Amazon decided. "That was what I had in mind. Certainly we're not going to let the Earth be destroyed by magna bombs if there's any way to prevent it… Start picking up speed, Abna. While the velocity is increasing we can have a meal, after which it will be a case of taking to our bunks and sleeping while the *Ultra* wings her way home through hyperspace on automatic control…"

* * * *

And the *Ultra* flew on… And still on, traveling through hyperspace. At last the instruments detected that the *Ultra* was approaching the solar system, and, entirely automatically, the ship dropped out of hyperspace, and the Crusaders were awakened. They hurried to the outlook window.

Infinitely far ahead on the edge of vision's furthest reach, there appeared a yellow pinpoint, which grew with the seconds. Instantly the analyzing telescope was turned upon it, and a quick reading made. "It's it!" the Amazon exulted. "Our sun! G-type dwarf, measuring up to all the facts we know about it. The Solar System itself will show up presently. Better reduce our speed, Abna."

This he was already doing, putting the power plant in reverse, using every ounce of that incredible energy to thrust away from their goal—and with the effort all the old symptoms of headlong acceleration returned, but this time it was deceleration with its attendant phenomenon of everlasting falling into a bottomless shaft.

The journey to Earth was swift and uneventful, and Abna swung the *Ultra* into an orbit about the planet.

"Evidently the magna-bombs haven't exploded yet,"

the Amazon said in relief. "Earth would be in pieces if that were so."

Abna nodded. "Where do you suggest I land? London, or go to your home and decide what we shall do?"

"We know what we're going to do; we don't need to go to my home to think that out. Head for London, and we'll start things moving at the Space Line headquarters. That's the best place and—let's hope that Chris Wilson is still there."

There was every chance that he might be. Chris Wilson was the Controller of World Spaceways—formerly the Dodd Space Line—and a dominant character of the Amazon's early life. Though he had probably become an old man in the time the quartet had been away, there was no reason why he should not be able to give them the information they wanted.

Abna did not ask any more questions. He brought the *Ultra* swiftly down through the atmosphere and then headed towards London, arriving over the city just as night had come. Silently reading the various directional beacons around the space and airports he continued on his way at a leisurely hundred miles an hour, finally choosing an untenanted space-ground on which to land. So huge was the *Ultra* it occupied all the space-ground as it settled down, an area usually estimated to house half a dozen big machines. Abna grinned as he switched off the power plant and turned.

"Probably be hearing rude words from the officials in a moment," he commented. "But if anybody has a right to land here, we have."

"Whatever comments they have we've no time for them," the Amazon answered. "Let's get into the Executive Building."

The Amazon depressed the airlock switch, and in a moment the heavy covering had slid silently back, revealing the old, familiar sky of Earth, and bringing in the warm softness of summer air. For some reason it seemed strange to vacate the *Ultra* and not have to be prepared for immediate dangers or atmospheric differences.

The Crusaders swept into the building. The Amazon was instantly recognized by amazed officials, but she ignored them as she hurried, unchallenged, to the elevator leading to Chris Wilson's executive offices.

"This will be Chris' biggest surprise to date, the Amazon murmured, tapping on the glass.

"Come in," requested a full, mature voice.

The Amazon stepped inside and the others followed her. Mexone, last of all, closed the door.

And at the big desk by the huge window, with the lights of London shining through it, a white-haired man still in the prime of physical condition, stared in blank amazement.

CHAPTER SEVEN
RACE AGAINST TIME

"Hello, Chris," the Amazon said, smiling, as she advanced slowly. "Bit of a surprise for you, eh?"

"Vi! By all that's wonderful!" Chris Wilson, fat and heavy and in the late sixties, jumped up from his chair and embraced her. "I just can't believe it! And you too, Abna... And Viona."

Still holding the Amazon in an endearing grip he shook hands in turn with Abna and Viona, and then looked at Mexone.

"Viona's husband, Mexone," the Amazon explained, disengaging herself. "Formerly an inhabitant of Voldas, a far distant planet."

"Delighted!" Chris shook hands and then asked, "And what have these three maniacs been doing to you, young man? Leading you the devil of a dance, I'll bet..." Chris turned back towards his desk, and looked at the Amazon.

"I'm going to call Ethel and Barry Schofield right away. As it happens, they're at home with my wife Ruth. Ethel in particular will be thrilled to see you again—and will want her daughter Rose to meet you too!" Chris smiled faintly. "She was born after you left, and has only ever seen you on television recordings. You're a legend in the family, Vi! Everyone will want to know where you've been, the things you've accomplished—"

"We've certainly been places, the Amazon admitted, "but I'm afraid I just haven't got time to meet your family. Don't call anyone. We didn't drop in here and nearly kill ourselves doing a lightning dash back from the deeps of space just to pass the time of day."

Chris turned away from the televisor on his desk, and looked his disappointment at the Amazon. "Then why are you here, Vi?"

"The entire Earth's in danger, Chris—real danger—and you might be the one to hurry things up if we're going to stop it."

"Danger? What sort of danger?"

"Total annihilation."

Chris Wilson knew the Amazon well enough to know she was not joking—and he also knew that nothing less than deadly danger would have brought her from her first love of space crusading.

"Sit down," he said quietly, nodding to chairs. "Now…" He sat again at the desk. "What's this all about?"

In detail the Amazon explained everything to him. His face became graver as he listened. "We've only got a few days to save things," the Amazon finished, "and at the moment we haven't the least idea where to start."

"Mmmm. The rest of your story is completely borne

out, you know. Until recently there has been one long story of murders, suicides, wars, strikes, and human disasters. Then they suddenly stopped, and I thought things had taken a better turn. Presumably it stopped because the only hypnosis at the moment are those in connection with the magna-bombs?"

"That would seem to be it," the Amazon agreed. "I thought we'd find the general hypnosis had ceased otherwise I was intending that we four should wear insulated helmets. It would seem that particular danger has passed."

"And a worse one remains," Chris mused. "Let me think now— The only clue I can give you is that General George Oliphant, in charge of Britain's defense forces, announced a few days ago that he was taking certain steps to safeguard Britain's interests against disaster."

"What disaster?" the Amazon asked pointedly.

"That I don't know. He was evasive, as these top brasshats usually are. That was all he said and nothing more has been heard about it since. I doubt if anybody even remembers the announcement. I certainly shouldn't have, had you not brought it back to mind."

"Seems to me we can count on him as one of the magna-bomb experts," Abna commented. "That leaves three others in different parts of the world. But how to find them? And quickly, too!"

"According to what the First said," the Amazon mused, "there arc four men at the four corners of the Earth—figuratively speaking—who are each planting bombs. And each one is doing it independently of the other. Apparently we have the British one in Gen. Oliphant, but he won't know about the other three. Tell you what to do Chris," she went on urgently, looking up. "While we get busy on Gen. Oliphant, you scour the news of the last few weeks for a similar announcement to that of Oliphant made by some foreign general or diplomat. In other words, trace as fast as possible— for our very lives depend on it—who else has suddenly decided to take 'defensive measures.' We'll keep in touch with you."

"Okay," Chris assented promptly, "but how secretive am I to be about this? In regard to the public and officials, I mean."

"There's no need to be secretive. Get your own staff onto it too. Just get the information, no matter what, and we'll do the rest..." The Amazon got to her feet. "Where's the best place to get hold of Oliphant?"

Chris opened a drawer and pulled forth a massive directory. He flipped the pages and studied them quickly.

"Here we are—Oliphant, Arthur. General of—"

"Never mind the decorations. What's the address?"

"The Cedars, Moorefield, Surrey." Chris reflected and then added, "Moorefield's a village just south of the Surrey by-pass road. You ought to have no difficulty in finding it."

"We won't," the Amazon said promptly. "Right! See you later."

* * * *

In silence the *Ultra* swept back and forth over the fields and villages, a monstrous dark shape against the stars. Cottages and residences there were in plenty, but to determine which one was the Cedars from a height of 2,000 feet was not so easy.

"We're wasting time," Abna said finally, peering below. "We'll have to land in a field and start walking."

"Yes, I suppose——" The Amazon stopped and snapped her fingers. "Wait a minute! Were definitely slipping in our judgment. There's a simple way."

As the others looked at her in surprise she hurried over to the instrument panel, talking as she went.

"These magna-bombs are being planted as the result of hypnotic orders, and those orders are being issued constantly from Kolb. That much we do know. They're only applicable, only capable of being absorbed by the four particular men who have been selected. Right so far?"

"Right, yes," Abna agreed, "but what good does it do us?"

"Plenty." The Amazon snapped on an instrument. "Many a time we've tested spatial vibration, so we can do it again. There will be a vibration in warped space as the hypnotic waves are issued through it. The spatial warp is the only medium in continuous contact with Kolb, far away as that planet is. At certain points the disturbance will reach a maximum due to the hypnotic waves passing through it. We must find that maximum disturbance and then get the tracer to work to point to the spot. That way we ought to find who's getting the waves—albeit unconsciously."

The spatial-vibration machine came into life as the Amazon finished talking. Upon the screen attached to it there was a dancing filigree of light.

"That's it," the Amazon murmured, studying it. "Some disturbance but not a great deal. Drive the *Ultra* around a bit, Abna, and we'll see what we get."

He did so, floating back and forth across the Surrey countryside so that he encompassed all its borders. The Amazon's eyes never left the vibratory detector, and at last she gave an order.

"That seems about the maximum disturbance. We crossed it before and got the same effect, but I wanted to make sure. Okay, let's see what happens."

Abna remained at the control board, hovering the *Ultra* so that it scarcely moved. Viona and Mexone watched intently as the Amazon pressed a button. Immediately a needle in universal mountings geared to the detector, oscillated quickly and then swung with its tip pointing diagonally downward.

"Good," the Amazon murmured. "My idea was right. The detector itself gives the extent of spatial vibration, and the extra disturbance at one point is caused by the hypnotic waves passing through it, all of which are directed to a point shown by this needle tip. Get going again, Abna. When the needle points directly downwards, that's the spot we want."

Abna nodded, dividing his attention between piloting the machine and watching the needle. At first it moved more into the horizontal as he went forward; so he reversed the vessel's flight, which had the required effect. Gradually the needle dipped, then at last became vertical, point downwards.

"That's it!" The Amazon switched the detector off, pressed the button actuating the shutter over the floor window. Intently the four peered down through the glass beneath their feet.

A lighter square was visible, surrounded by a thick darkness that was probably trees. Beyond this obscurity lay the general dim gray of the countryside proper.

"It's a house—of sorts," the Amazon said. "Probably one of those big ones in which brasshats choose to live."

"We can find out by the searchlight," Viona said, but before she could stride to the switchboard the Amazon caught her arm.

"We don't want it, Viona. Give too much warning. If the General's there we don't want him running away... Drop down to the country, Abna—near as you reasonably can to the house without flattening it."

In five minutes it was done. Abna switched off the power plant and stood waiting.

"The rest is common-or-garden breaking and entering," the Amazon said. "The General has got to tell us things, and since he does not know he is under hypnotic influence we don't want to make him too uncomfortable."

"Shouldn't the hypnotic influence affect anybody coming within range of it?" Mexone asked. "Ourselves, for instance?"

The Amazon shook her head. "It's tuned to the

particular minds of the men concerned. I'm not quite sure how such a feat is accomplished, but I imagine that with duplicates of the men on Earth 2 an analysis of their brains, and the type of vibration which would affect them, would be possible... The scientists of Kolb arc no fools," the Amazon sighed, thinking. "And we haven't nearly finished battling with them yet."

She glanced at Abna as she realized he was not paying much attention to her words, He was busy now at the long metal bench where the machine tools were fitted. One of them was whirring, busily fashioning a light affair of thin metal, circular in shape.

"What's the idea?" the Amazon asked.

"Insulation cap," Abna answered. "It will make our job easier if the hypnosis is cut off from the general."

The Amazon nodded, conscious of surprise that she had not thought of the idea herself; but then her mind had been on other things. It was typical of Abna to fill in the blank spaces she had left.

The job finished, the Amazon led the way outside. The others followed her, locking the *Ultra* from the outside, though this was probably a needless precaution. Then, completely silent under the stars they advanced toward the big, light-colored, detached house nearby. The only signs of life about it came from a downstairs room. The big windows were brightly lighted, the rays streaming across a well-kept lawn. Passing though the gateway, the four paused and surveyed, alert for a possible dog that might give warning. As it happened, all remained quiet.

"I presume that's the general at the head of the table," the Amazon murmured. "Dining with his family... Hmm, we'll have to put up with that, I suppose."

Abna nodded, studying the scene before him. A florid, soldierly looking man was eating steadily, meanwhile exchanging conversation with a graying, good-looking woman—possibly his wife—and a much younger woman with a pretty face and black hair. The only assumption was that it was his daughter.

"Mexone and I will deal with the women," Viona said. "You two concentrate on the general. We're ready when you are."

The Amazon did not hesitate any longer. She jerked her head to Abna, strode across the lawn, and up to the French windows. They opened easily as she pressed down the catch. She walked into the brightly lighted room with its comfortable furniture and well-laid table, Abna immediately behind her... The two women and the man stared fixedly, dumfounded.

"And what the devil's the meaning of this?" the man demanded at last, his fierce blue eyes popping.

The women did not say anything. They were staring in fascination at the black costumes of the quartet, and particularly at the great stature of Abna the insulated head-cover in his hand.

"General Oliphant?" the Amazon asked briefly, and the man nodded.

"Yes, I'm General Oliphant. What do you want?"

"A private conversation." The Amazon glanced at Viona and Mexone. "All right—you two deal with the ladies."

"Now look here—" the general roared, jumping to his feet; but he promptly sat down again under the immense pressure of Abna's hands. Fuming, he watched as his wife and daughter were quite courteously ushered into an adjoining room; then the door closed.

"Explain yourself!" Oliphant barked. "And make it good before I have the law on you. Who are you? Damned space travelers, I suppose?"

"The Cosmic Crusaders, to be exact," the Amazon answered. "And you have no need for worry. Your wife and daughter—as I presume they are—won't be harmed in the least. And neither will you."

Then she became silent before the general's blast of wrath as Abna put the insulated covering on top of his bristly head.

"What in thunder are you doing? Take this infernal thing off my head!"

"It is better that it stays here," Abna said quietly, holding it firmly. "My wife will explain why."

Oliphant glared at the Amazon. "Well, why?"

"To business, general," the Amazon said, and her very tone showed that she meant it. "Quite recently you conceived the idea of placing a magna-bomb in a certain place for defense purposes. Where is that place?"

The general hesitated, his brows knitted. He seemed to be struggling with something in his mind.

"I'll tell you something," the Amazon continued.

"And every word of it is truth. You have been under hypnotic orders for some time now—including the time when you supposedly thought up the idea of planting the magna-bomb. At the moment that hypnotic power has no effect on you, because of the insulated covering resting on your head."

Oliphant stared, then he laughed derisively. "Hypnotic power! There isn't a soul on Earth who could hypnotize me. I've too strong a will for that."

"The responsible body isn't on Earth, but operating through machines many light centuries away," the Amazon said patiently. "It is too long a story to explain, but I give you my word that it is true. There is deadly danger in this bomb you have planted. Where is its hiding place?"

Again the general seemed to reflect; then said slowly:

"Do you know, I think your story of hypnosis may be right. For the first time in weeks I feel different, more the master of myself than I have been feeling... I am even wondering why I planted that bomb at all. Yet I felt determined to do it. I made a long speech to the press, and then—"

"Where is it?" the Amazon asked deliberately. "Tell us, general. There isn't a moment to lose."

He went across to the nearby bureau, selected a sheet of paper, and then drew a sketch of the countryside with military accuracy.

"Here," he said, indicating two squares, "are military depots. Not very big ones—little more than camps—but they're plain enough from the air and the road. Those detachments are under my control. Now, between them, in this long stretch of pasture land between the two camps is the location of the bomb. It is buried at a depth of three feet. There are no signs or notices to show where it is."

"When was the bomb timed to explode?" the Amazon demanded.

"Midnight, July 10."

"And it's July 8 now," Abna said grimly, glancing at the bureau calendar. "We've got to move fast, Vi. The other bombs will all go off at the same time."

"We're off this moment," the Amazon said; then she glanced again at the general, the insulating covering still on his head. "Thanks for everything, general. We'll deal with it."

"Why don't I come with you? Save you time searching."

The Amazon picked up the sketch from the bureau. "No need for that. Magna-bombs reveal themselves immediately on detectors. We'll find it all right. Your job is to stay here and not say a word about this interview you've had with us, not even to your wife and daughter. If any information leaks out, it may warn the other bomb-planters and that in turn will increase our difficulties."

The Amazon wasted no further time. She nodded a farewell and then headed for the French windows with the others behind her. In a few moments they were back in the *Ultra*.

"Ascend no higher than one hundred feet, Abna,"

she instructed, looking at the sketch in her hand. "I'll operate the Geiger detector. It shouldn't take us very long to find that radioactive nuisance."

Abna obeyed. The power plant hummed and the *Ultra* lifted to the required height of one hundred feet. Then it sped forward, slowly and silently, over grassland and valleys, over hedges, cottages and rivers, the Amazon constantly checking the sketch and also operating the supersensitive Geiger counter apparatus. Presently, as the directions of the sketch were faithfully followed, the counter began to click, slowly and intermittently. The Amazon looked up and ahead through the observation window.

"We're on to it," she said briefly. "Those white smudges in the dark are the army encampments... Right! Bring us down before we're too close to them."

Abna cut the power and the *Ultra* descended to rolling, deserted grassland. No time was wasted. The airlock was still open—there had been no need to close it for such a short, airborne journey. Picking up a portable Geiger counter apparatus, the Amazon led the way outside, the others behind her... After which it was not a difficult job to trace the hidden bomb. The Geiger counter gave away its position almost immediately.

"What do you intend doing?" Abna asked, as they all stood in a group around the vital spot.

"Defusing it," the Amazon answered simply. "Then we'll take it away in the *Ultra* with us."

"It's a terrific risk," Viona pointed out seriously.

"I'm aware of it." The Amazon handed the now silent Geiger apparatus to Abna and then felt around in the soft ground with her hands. It was not long before she encountered something solid and metallic. Carefully she began to scoop away the soil and in dead silence, not able to see much under the misty stars, the others stood watching.

With infinite care the Amazon removed the main calibrated outer screw and exposed the fuse itself— a long, slender rod of polished copper, which was engaging with softly ticking mechanism within. Her task was to remove the rod, and the slightest variation from side to side could prematurely actuate the mechanism and fire the bomb.

She dried her palms quickly on her suit and controlling every nerve and movement of her body, she began to edge the rod slowly upwards, taking care it did not move from side to side in its narrow neck. Once it slipped ever so slightly and grazed the side. There was an awful pause, but nothing happened. The Amazon tried again, and at last had the fuse out, like a dully gleaming of dipstick in the starlight. She released her breath thankfully and then listened. The soft ticking had ceased.

"Right; it's harmless," she said. "Get it out while I recover myself."

With rapid speed Abna, Viona and Mexone finished the job, digging the now harmless cylinder out of its hiding place. The Amazon led the way back to the *Ultra*, the firing fuse in her hand. Once within the ship she put the fuse in the power plant matrix, where its copper could be of some, if only slight, use.

"And now?" Abna asked, returning from the storage chamber where he had placed the bomb. "Three more to go. How do we set about it?"

"We contact Chris and see if he's anything to tell us. If not, we use the spatial-vibration machine to find our men. All we can do."

She turned to the radio and switched it on, finally adjusting to the closed circuit wavelength of Chris Wilson's office. After a moment his voice came over the loudspeaker.

"World Spaceways—Wilson speaking."

"Vi here, Chris. How much did you find out, if anything? We've dealt with the Oliphant bomb, and now we're ready for the others."

"Good! I'm afraid the only details I can give you aren't very explicit. I've managed to discover the countries in which the announcements were made, together with the names of the men who made the announcements, but that's all."

"Let's have them," the Amazon requested.

"There was D'Alvarez, the Brazilian diplomat, who made his announcement in Buenos Aires. Then there was Denson, the Australian military man, who did the same in Melbourne. And finally there was Frudinoff, the Russian war minister. Who made his announcement from Novaya Zemlya, of all places."

The Amazon's hand ceased writing on a scratch pad. "Right, Chris, thanks. We've got a rough idea of where to look, and I fancy that our instruments will take care of the rest of it. When we've finished our various hops we'll be in touch with you again. By the way, deadline is midnight on July 10."

CHAPTER EIGHT
THE END OF KOLB

The Amazon turned from the radio and looked at the others grimly. "Set the course for South America, Abna."

He promptly complied, and the *Ultra* started immediately to climb to the stratosphere where atmospheric resistance was at a minimum. Once the rarefied heights were reached the huge vessel turned southwestwards and flew with phenomenal speed across the Atlantic Ocean, arriving over the South American coast when it was still dark.

This set the pattern of experience for several hours to come. The same procedure was adopted as in England. First the person concerned was traced by the spatial-vibration machine—then no matter where he was, or what he was doing, the four descended on him. A hypnosis insulator-cap was provided once again, made by Abna during the trip, and the same methods as with General Oliphant were followed. In the case of D'Alvarez there was not much difficulty. He was in bed when the four found him, in the suite of a Buenos Aires hotel. The four made entry by the roof emergency fire escape, leaving the *Ultra* on empty land a few miles away from the city. Once, the details were in hand the bomb was sought for, near the Gulf of St. Matias, and duly found and rendered harmless.

Without a pause the four carried on, working now against time. With its usual vast velocity, taking to outer space this time to avoid frictional difficulty, the *Ultra* made the journey to daylit Australia in a matter of twenty minutes, and once again the same detection method was used. Denson was in the company of four political men when the quartet located him. Quietly they were disposed of—rendered insensible by anesthetic for some hours to come—and Denson was forced, not very willingly, to give up the facts. Yet again a hypnosis insulator was provided, and finally the truth came out. The bomb itself was near Brisbane, and in one hour it was located and the fuse removed.

So to Novaya Zemlya and the frozen expanses of the Arctic ocean. Here there was not so much good fortune facing the quartet. They got no spatial ether vibration out of Novaya Zemlya. The Russian diplomat might have made his speech there, but evidently he had moved since to parts unknown. Then began an almost frantic search, criss-crossing the immeasurable wastes of Russia at high velocity. Literally hours were lost, until at last there was a growing spatial reaction over a small town near the Urals on the shores of the Caspian sea.

Here at last Frudinoff was located, enjoying a fishing holiday at a lonely shack. The solitariness of his position made him an easy man to tackle, but against that there was his Russo-Mongolian stubbornness to break down. To this end the hypnosis insulator only partly helped. Finally his mind had to be read by Abna before the truth could be obtained.... The bomb was in Novaya Zemlya itself.

At five o'clock in the afternoon of that frantic day the last bomb was defused and removed. Only then did Abna turn the *Ultra* back on a course set for Britain. He was smiling in satisfaction.

"Well, Vi, that's that," he said. "We've done our job."

"Part of it," the Amazon corrected, musing as she gazed down on sprawling Russia far below.

"Part of it?" Abna repeated. "I don't quite follow."

The Amazon turned and looked at him, then at Viona and Mexone.

"It should be obvious to all of you that things don't end here," she said. "In fact they can't. Though the Denafrone—what's left of it after our activities—have no longer got a duplicate Earth by which to study conditions here, they'll certainly find out somehow what's happened, and then the fun will begin all over again. The Denafrone have somehow got to destroy Earth because in time Earthlings can become a danger to them. We found that out long ago. There's only one answer to that—destroy the Denafrone. Get our blow in first."

"We discussed that some time ago and got no further," Abna pointed out. "We can't destroy the Denafrone without also destroying those who've been enslaved by them. And that wouldn't be fair to them."

"I said before that there might be a way, but that I wanted to think about it," the Amazon replied slowly. "I have thought about it, and we're going to get some action—ruthless action, but nonetheless effective." She made a decisive movement. "First we'll tell Chris that the bomb effort has succeeded—we can advise him by radio to save time—and then we're going back into space."

"Space? For how far?" Abna questioned.

"To within a few million miles of Kolb— Yes, yes, I know what you're thinking," the Amazon added, as she saw the amazed faces. "We shall again have to endure a vast journey. Again we shall have to fore-shorten time and distance by turning off into hyper-space. Fact remains, it's got to be done."

"Might I ask why?" Abna questioned seriously.

"Purely so that we can advise the slave-workers of danger, and give them every chance to get out before their planet is destroyed. That girl Silda told us of a closed radio circuit among the workers with a wave-length of four six two. Naturally, a radio message sent from Earth here would take hundreds of years to arrive, so it has to be sent from within a reasonable distance of the planet. That is what we're going to do. For no other reason than to give the workers a chance. Fortunately, you know the language, Abna, so you can send the message."

* * * *

Once the Amazon had advised Chris Wilson of the success of the bomb search, she added that she and the others were leaving Earth for approximately a month. She gave no indication of her destination, merely saying that there was much yet to be done... About this Chris did not argue. He had learned from experience never to question the decisions of this extraordinary superwoman.

And, as night was closing down on the western hemisphere of Earth, the *Ultra* fled once more into the deeps of space, and again piled velocity on velocity as she hurtled toward the hazy enormity of the Milky Way.

A week of Earth time passed. Ten days. Thirteen days passed, and at this point the *Ultra* began to automatically emerge from hyperspace. The controls pre-set, its speed was commencing to noticeably drop as the four emerged from unconsciousness to an awareness of what was happening.

As they began to take up the threads of reasoning again they climbed from their bunks and went to the observation window. There, before them, was the vast swirling scum of light, of planets and stars, which formed the First Galaxy.

"We're near enough to send a radio message," the Amazon said, glancing at Abna. "If we get too close the Denafrone might get sight of us—or at least detect us."

Abna took over the radio, and the Amazon the switchboard. And while he intoned steadily in the

Kolbian language, the Amazon set the instruments to work to chart the course back to the solar system. In time the still fast speeding *Ultra* slowly changed direction, the enormous mass of the First Galaxy seeming to swing around while the vessel remained apparently still—

Then, suddenly, an answering call from the loudspeaker. The Amazon glanced around, then signaled to Viona.

"Set these switches, Viona: I've work to do. Moving to Abna's side, the Amazon continued: "Tell them to get spaceships by any means they can and make good their escape to a neighboring world. Say we are friends of the slave Silda who met her death escaping from the Denafrone. Make it clear that about a month will elapse before Kolb's destroyed, and that when it comes if will be very sudden and without further warning… Under no circumstances are the facts to get to the Denafrone."

Abna translated rapidly, then sat listening to the reply. When it had concluded, he spoke the equivalent of "Farewell!" and switched off.

"I spoke to one of the workers who is in some sort of position of authority," he explained. "He seemed to doubt the warning at first, but I think I convinced him in the finish. He's going to make every effort to save himself and his people."

"Then we can't do any more," the Amazon said. "We'll get a meal, have a brief relaxation, and then commence the long journey home once more."

This was duly done, and by the time the meal was over

the *Ultra* had almost completely turned in a half circle and was commencing once more to build up slowly to a speed approaching that of light before plunging into hyperspace. In that way their great initial velocity would ensure the fastest possible transit in hyperspace.

"Before we are compelled to rest," Abna said, looking across at the Amazon, "what precisely do you intend doing to destroy Kolb? You spoke of turning the spatial vibration back on itself, with disastrous results to Kolb."

"Exactly. That there will be a disaster I ascertained beforehand from the First. You will have grasped, I suppose, that enormous agitation of the fabric of space-time—which extends from one side of the expanding Universe to the other, if one can say such a thing of something that is circular—is being created by the Denafrone. Primarily, this agitation carried reflected light waves, hypnotic waves, and all manner of waves necessary for the duplication of Earth. More recently the agitation has been—and still is being—used for the conveyance of four separate hypnosis vibrations, so devised that they follow their recipients—the concealers of the magna-bombs—wherever they might be. The machines of Kolb, ruled by the Denafrone, are still at work causing an immense channel or warp in space, which channel carries the various vibrations of which I've spoken. Clear so far?"

"Go on," Abna invited, thinking.

"Imagine this channel in space! The Denafrone machines are using carefully planned vibrations to force this channel in what is normally a smooth, intangible sea. Vast power is being used to produce the effect. It is as though there was a big rubber sheet, and machines are forcing a V-shaped wedge, under immense stress, down the center of it. It is strained to the limit in order to permit the various hypnosis waves and so forth to have an unimpeded passage at ultra-light speeds. What happens when an opposing force at the other end of this channel breaks the tension?"

"Presumably space-time will snap back into its normal position, making a huge universal ripple which will travel to the outermost bounds of the Universe."

"Exactly so—but there's something else, too. The Denafrone machines will receive back into themselves a force exactly consistent with the force they are exerting. They will blow apart with shattering violence—violent enough, as I see it, though I've yet to check it, to smash the entire planet in pieces. Imagine a machine using enormous energy to produce, say, a single steady output of vibration. Imagine that vibration suddenly blocked and turned back along the same track into the machine that created it. Instant destruction would be the result. It is just another aspect of the age-old fact that two bodies cannot occupy the same space at the same time."

"I see what you mean," Abna said slowly. "And the energy is bound to go back to the machines because it will follow exactly the course along which it has been originally transmitted..." Then as the Amazon nodded, a thought seemed to strike him. "But surely it will take years? Think of the distance between Earth and Kolb!"

"It will be almost instantaneous. The First said that light—and that equally means any vibration—is not limited to 186,000 miles a second when it is controlled mechanically and enhanced, using fourth dimensional properties. He got results almost instantly without time-lag, therefore, those same forces will still be operating and will make the retraction just as fast as the transmission. The very machines which are governing the radiations—making them travel almost instantaneously—will also govern the retraction at the same rate."

There was a silence and the four looked at each other; then attention became focused on the Amazon herself in silent admiration for the scientific reprisal she had devised.

"It's clever," Abna admitted; "yet even so, it is still only a brilliant theory. Do you mind if I submit it to the computers and see if they decide it's practical?"

"Not at all. I was going to do that in any case. In fact, I'll do it myself, then I can feed the machines with the basic figures."

The Amazon got to her feet and Abna followed her example. Together they went across to the bank of computers. Then she gave each machine a different aspect of the problem to solve. In response they hummed and glowed, their incredibly complicated interiors working at top pressure to provide the flawless answer of the postulations that had been fed into them.

One by one the Amazon examined them, then the others came to her side and looked over her shoulder. As she came to the last one she gave a smile of triumph.

"So you were right!" Abna exclaimed, perusing them. "Good work, Vi! And right here you've got the formula worked out. The vibration necessary to create the repulsive force. It's going to need some mighty complicated wiring diagrams."

"There are no better scientific engineers than those of Earth," the Amazon said, with a rare touch of pride. "That is, under the right supervision. We're returning to Earth fast as we can, and once there we'll marshal all the necessary labor and draw up designs for machines. It's only justice, since Earth people have been made to dance to the Denafrone tune, that they should be the ones to have the final answer...."

"There's just one final point about this which I'd like answering," Abna said. "If we destroy Kolb—or I should say when we destroy Kolb—it will be visible, won't it?"

"Of course. If what I think is correct, it will become like a brief flaming nova, a sudden star flaring in the Milky Way, then it will vanish forever."

Abna sighed. "That's a pity. Generations will pass before it can be seen. Think of the time-factor. The light waves won't reach us for hundreds of years."

"Mmm. I'd overlooked that," the Amazon admitted. "But you're quite right. The light waves, not being machine governed, will travel back to us at normal speed. That will mean centuries hence before there's any visible sign of what we've done."

"We've got time-travel apparatus on board this ship, which we've used many times before," Viona remarked. "There's nothing to stop us going to the scene of the explosion, then turning back in Time to view it."

"Never a dull moment," Abna smiled. "That's the answer, Viona."

* * * *

Yet again the *Ultra* fled back to Earth, devouring the billions of spatial miles and light years with never a flaw in her humming power plant. Yet again hyperspace was traversed, and yet again the mighty vessel emerged into normal space with the Earth solar system's outskirts just visible. From then on the quartet came back to life, organized themselves, and at length looked down on the green speck that was Earth.

In a matter of two hours they had reached it, arriving in London as daylight was fully established. As before, they settled down at the World Space Corporation's grounds and went in search of Chris Wilson. As usual he was at his post and he did not seem too surprised when the four entered his great office."

"You come and go, and no questions asked," he commented. "Where have you been in the last few weeks?"

"Back to Kolb," the Amazon said briefly. "Tipping off the slaves there of danger to come."

Chris stared. "You mean to tell me you made that fantastic trip just to tell them that?"

"Certainly. Don't forget it's a matter of life and death to them. Anyway, what's the difference? Be it the moon or Kolb, it's only a journey anyhow. One gets a new perspective on distance when traveling in the *Ultra*... However, I'll tell you what happened."

Sitting down, the Amazon explained every detail with occasional comments from one or other of the party. Chris listened in fascinated silence. He always did when he absorbed the exploits of the Amazon. As an ordinary man, her fantastic behavior was something that always made him curiously silent and overwhelmed.

"So that's the situation to date," the Amazon concluded. "Our job now is to get the necessary machinery assembled to give these Denafrone scientists a taste of their own medicine."

"There isn't a simpler way?" Chris asked, musing, and the Amazon shook her head.

"No. Even if there were, I wouldn't take it. The Denafrone are a deadly breed, Chris, and even if they're balked for now they are not stopped. In time they will become an even greater problem. The only answer is their destruction. I know what I'm talking about."

"Of course. You always do. Well, rely on me for co-operation. What do you want me to do?"

"Not much you can do, really: our chief reason for coming was to keep you in touch with things. Our task from now on is to see what the various government authorities can do. We need engineers, labor, materials, and so forth."

The prime minister was interviewed, but there was cold, obstinate refusal to do anything. Baffled, and decidedly annoyed, the Amazon had finally to retire. When she and the others reached the *Ultra* once more after their peregrinations she was in a decidedly bad tamper.

"What's the matter with him?" she demanded. "It makes you wonder why we ever bothered to save the Earth at all! Not only from the bombs, but on many past occasions. Gratitude! I even offer to finance everything, and they won't listen!"

"Perhaps," Abna said slowly, "there's a good reason?"

"There couldn't be."

Abna did not pursue the subject, nor did he explain himself. Instead he went over to the spatial-vibration detector and switched it on. After a moment or two he pointed to the screen on which was a vivid tracery of oscillation.

"What do you make of that?" he asked grimly, and the Amazon's brows knitted as she stared at the screen.

"I don't quite know. That looks as though there's considerable spatial disturbance at work—yet there shouldn't be. The only place where the disturbance should be apparent is in the regions where the four bomb messengers are located, and then it's because of hypnosis waves."

"Suppose," Abna said grimly, "general hypnosis is here again, the same as before? The hypnosis that caused crimes, suicides, and war?"

"But the Denafrone can't know we're planning to destroy their planet!" the Amazon protested. "So why stir up everybody against us?"

"They can know—and probably do. That radio message we sent on a closed circuit was intended for the workers, but how do we know but what the Denafrone had tabs on it? It's possible they heard every word we said, or else have deduced the facts since.... In fact," he said, thinking, "that's probably what's happened. Presumably the slaves have seized spaceships and began an exodus to one of their neighboring worlds. Obviously the Denafrone will be aware of that. Yes, we'd better assume that they know we have said Kolb is to be destroyed. They know full well Earthlings couldn't do that in the normal way—but with us behind them it would be a different matter. We might conceivably carry out our threat.... What to do al»out it? Stir up Earthlings against us, and probably try to make them kill us."

"If we accept your theory—which has a horrible ring of possibility about it," the Amazon said slowly, "let's try some other facts as well. If there's general hypnosis at work, why aren't we affected by it ourselves?"

"Chiefly, I think, because we spend so much time in the *Ultra*, which has insulated walls. The hypnosis waves may penetrate in time, but there'll certainly be a delay. With the ordinary folk living in a normal way it's different."

"There doesn't seem to be much the matter with Chris Wilson," Mexone pointed out. "He was only too willing to help."

"He was at that time," Abna answered. "Our difficulties began when we left him. First the obstinate under-official, culminating in the cold refusal of the P.M., whom we know is really a benign and helpful man.... The hypnotic influence must have begun about the time we left Chris Wilson."

The Amazon clenched her yellow fists. "Then this means that wherever we go on Earth we'll get no help."

Abna sat down and meditated, blind and deaf to everything save his own thoughts. By force of circumstances, leadership of the quartet had passed to him, and perhaps it was as well.

Though there was no limit to the Amazon's brilliant scientific conceptions, she was not one for organized planning. Savage, instant action was her usual method, whereas Abna believed in careful plotting.

"We have two advantages," he said finally. "First, we can make headgear to completely insulate ourselves from whatever influence there might be, and second, we have a vessel which is proof against any attack Earthlings can devise... There's only one way out of this. Design the machines we want ourselves, manufacture them ourselves, and install them somewhere ourselves. Some quiet spot. Whatever opposition there is we'll crush. I don't like hitting at Earthlings, but since it's for the good of the majority, it can't be helped."

"We can design the machinery, but the manufacture of it may take weeks, even months," the Amazon protested. "We needed the labor to get the thing done quickly."

"I know. It simply means we shan't be as quick, but we'll certainly be as sure. Okay—we know what we're doing. First move is to get out into space away from interruptions and get the designs worked out. You two, Viona and Mexone, can manufacture head coverings for us. That's settled."

Abna did not delay any further. He glanced at the still closed airlock and then started up the power plant. In another moment or two the *Ultra* was climbing to the heights. And it kept on climbing until it had reached a point midway between Earth and Moon. Here Abna put the vessel into a vast orbit about the Earth.

"While you're making those helmets," he said to the younger ones, "keep a sharp lookout. If yon see any spaceships from Earth, inform us right away... Now, Vi, let's get busy."

It was roughly three meals and two short sleeps later before the machinery was finished on paper.

Many of the original ideas had undergone modification, mainly so that everything could be placed in the smallest possible mechanical area—and also so that the *Ultra*'s own machine tools were capable of tackling the manufacture.

"That about settles it," Abna said finally. "We can get back to Earth and start the manufacture."

"What exactly have you devised?" Viona asked curiously.

"The computers suggested a vibration twice as strong as that used by the Denafrone to force the space-warp channel," the Amazon said. "So we're adopting the suggestion. When that vibration is released into the space it will force the incoming vibration back on itself. It will, to put it metaphorically, telescope. It will be suddenly unable to progress and the effect on the machines of the Denafrone will be disastrous."

"For our power we need a special outside generator," Abna said. "One of the type using water power will be sufficient."

"Why can't we carry out the whole operation from within the *Ultra*?" Mexone asked, frowning.

"Because there are simply too many competing energy fields on board our ship, despite its screening," the Amazon explained. "We're using very precisely calculated forces, and for that we need to be outside of the ship, where the insulated hull will be sufficient to cut off any stray radiations. And," the Amazon added, moving to the switchboard, "if there's opposition, we'll soon deal with it. Now let's get back and start operations."

She set the controls and started the *Ultra* moving forward. To reach Earth it was only a small hop. As they neared the planet the Amazon cut in the invisibility screen, to confound any watchers on Earth, and in less than an hour the journey was accomplished. Swiftly the machine, still invisible, came down, crossed the lusher regions of South America, and eventually settled in sunlit foothills of the Peruvian Andes. Abruptly the *Ultra* became visible as Abna switched off the invisibility screen, now no longer needed.

"There's the river we want," Abna said, pointing through the window. "And as for being deserted, I don't think we could find a better spot than this."

He was right. On every hand there stretched barren waste. The vegetated regions began toward the eastern horizon: as for the rest, it was mainly sun-parched, rocky, and partly desert, the only sign of coolness existing in the nearby river which plunged and foamed from the mountain heights, until, at this point, it was a decidedly swift and dangerous current.

"To work!" Abna said decisively. "There's much to be done."

Promptly work began. The machine tools were set to work, and the labor of construction got under way. First the generator was made, in sections, and as each section was completed it was transferred to a point near the river's edge, using the *Ultra* as the crane by which to accomplish the heavier haulage.

For a week the four worked on, as uninterrupted as if they were on some distant planet. There was nothing but the sunlight, the occasional clouds of stinging dust, and the slowly forming generator on the riverbank. This latter duty was the job of Viona and Mexone, and their engineering skill proved quite sufficient to the task.

"We've done it all quicker than we expected," the Amazon commented, when the final check-over was complete. "Our tests show everything to be in order, so I suggest we release the 'Repulser' before night sets in... Now, to be precise."

"Okay," Abna agreed, along with Viona and Mexone standing nearby.

"Ready?" Abna questioned.

"Yes, of course," said the Amazon.

Her eyes traveled over the dusty, sunlit spaces, and finally to the surging river nearby, its powerful current turning the specially designed blades of the generator. A button clicked on the switch-panel beneath her fingers and, slowly, the generator started to function, first with a faint humming note and finally with a deep bass roaring as the full effect of the rushing river came into being.

The second switch moved, controlling the 'Repulser'. Only the various pilot-lights showed that it was operating, otherwise there was nothing visible. Connected to the generator, it steadily rose to full output, hurling its repulsive energy skywards in an ever-widening fan, so devised that it would form a barrier some millions of miles wide when it reached outer space, and thereby form a complete 'wall' against the incoming waves from Kolb.

"And that's all there is to it," the Amazon said shouting over the roar of the generator. "We can't behold anything unless we travel into space and sidetrack Time... And I think that's what we'd better do, even as Viona suggested. We need to be absolutely certain that Kolb has been destroyed."

"And what happens if an attempt is made to destroy this lot?" Abna asked. "The Denafrone may see it, and compel people on Earth to launch an attack. We've gotten away with things so far, but it's probably only a matter of time."

"It won't signify," the Amazon answered. "The repulsion wave has been generated. The longer the machine runs the stronger it will become, but even if it were cut off now, we've released enough power to do the trick. The 'rebound' effect has probably already happened. Our machine can either be destroyed, or run itself to pieces... Our job is done." She cast a last look around he deserted spaces and then turned toward the *Ultra*. "Let's be on our way."

* * * *

In the space of an hour the *Ultra*, with ever-mounting speed, had reached the orbit of Mars and, picking up velocity with every second, flashed onwards to the limits of the Solar System, and beyond that again into the Greater Deeps.

Calmly the four settled themselves for the journey, and when at length all automatics were set they allowed themselves to relapse into unconsciousness. And in this state they remained while the light centuries passed and hyper-space was traversed. Then again the warning bells sounded in their ears. The vessel was slowing down by robot controls. Gradually the four returned to their senses to find themselves once more with the hazy mystery of the Milky Way filling all space before them.

"All seems to be in order," Abna said, after a survey of the instruments. "And we're slowing down fast. The spectra of the sun in that solar system ahead checks with that of Kolb. A check of the planets shows that Kolb seems to be missing—but we need to be certain. More particularly, we need to know that the Denafrone didn't escape into space before the disintegration."

"I don't see how they could," Mexone mused. "If the slaves rose up and commandeered the spaceships before they realized what was happening, they'd have no means of doing so."

"We've arrived some way behind the instant when Kolb was destroyed," the Amazon said. "That's obvious, since we worked out that the destruction would be almost instantaneous. Therefore, what we need to do is work out on the computers the exact time from now to the moment when we released the repulsive force. Once we know that we'll traverse Time backwards to shortly before that point."

She turned to the computers and set to work. She read the figures they gave, nodded to herself, and then set the time controls to the same reading.

The controls set, she pulled the main delayed-action switch. Then moving to the center of the control room, she waited with the others for the effect she knew had to come.

Presently it came—a strange conviction of lurching, of turning inside out. Outside the observation window the stars went through weird gyrations as Time changed and they with them. Then, gradually, the sensations passed and space became still again.

The Amazon glanced across at the Time apparatus

as, with a click, it ceased to function.

"That's it," she said. "We're occupying the Time when we released the repulsion on Earth. We've emerged just outside of Kolb's system because of stellar drift, but we should still be near enough to see what we came for. If that effect was instantaneous, we ought to see something happen."

They waited, the *Ultra* cruising at high speed, heading towards the Kolbian system, but their speed was not high enough to bring them visibly nearer to the vast sea of the Milky Way itself. In silence they grouped around the window, watching intently through protective goggles the cold, diamond-glitter of the stars and suns. Somewhere amidst all that maze was far-flung Kolb, the planet written down for destruction.

Minutes passed—and then suddenly a change. A pale speck, no more than eighth magnitude, and situated amidst a backdrop of stars, suddenly flared like ignited magnesium. In a few seconds it climbed from eighth magnitude to first, blazing away like an incredible sun amidst the hosts which surrounded it.

"That's it," the Amazon breathed. "Kolb burning up, being consumed, and everything with it. The last stand of the Denafrone indeed…"

For close on half an hour the quartet watched the death of a world millions of miles away.

They watched the incredible blaze gradually die down until it expired altogether. There was no longer anything there. Yet so slight had Kolb's gravity been in relation to the surrounding stars, there was not the slightest trace of any shifting of balance.

Nor were there any shock gravity waves. The *Ultra* would have rocked had there been any, but the mighty vessel sailed serenely onwards. "And now?" Abna asked, at length.

"We keep going toward that point and see what remains there are," the Amazon said. "Just to satisfy ourselves."

"I've a better idea," Abna remarked, and moved to the radio apparatus. To the Amazon's surprise, he began intoning in the Kolbian language, broadcasting across a wide range of frequencies. Presently a jabber of alien speech came from the speaker. Abna spoke briefly, then switched off. Smiling faintly, he turned to the Amazon.

"Well?" the Amazon demanded, irritably. "Who were you talking to? It sounded like the Denafrone, and if so—"

"Relax, Vi! I was talking to one of the leaders of the former slaves. He confirmed to me that most of them had managed to escape into space, leaving the Denafrone marooned on their own planet. Apparently security was pretty lax in the wake of the confusion caused by our killing the First and others of the ruling clique. They've settled on a couple of the habitable planets in their system, including Earth 2, which has now stabilized into a virgin world ready for them to take over."

"Well, that's that! I think we should have a meal," Viona said brightly, giving a signal to Mexone. "A special meal, too, in celebration of a job well done."

The Amazon and Abna watched them hurry out of the control room to begin their preparations. After a moment or two he put an arm about her shoulders.

"We're backwards in Time, don't forget," he said. "Hadn't we better advance to normal?"

The Amazon shrugged. "No need, is there? Out here, Time values count for very little."

Abna was silent for a moment, then he said: "We could go back to Earth if you want. Now the hypnosis powers of the Denafrone are ended, Earth people will be normal again."

"True, but— Back to Earth and do what?" the Amazon asked; then she gave a faint smile and added: "I couldn't help but think, in the brief time we were on Earth, how immensely tedious it all seemed compared to sweeping Space and tackling an endless series of problems. We're not cut out to live and die on one planet, Abna. Neither are Mexone or Viona. Space is our home…"

She paused, frowning as she looked through the observation window. Abna, following her gaze, looked also and then he gave a start. Things were not as they had been a little while ago.

In the blank space which the destroyed Kolb had left behind there had appeared four glittering points, set in such a way they resembled the points of the compass. The top and bottom points were set above each other in a direct line; and the same applied for the 'left' and 'right' points. And each point was a different color.

The top was bright emerald, the bottom ruby red, the left-hand one was sapphire blue and the right-hand one a golden yellow.

"Where did they come from?" the Amazon asked in amazement. "What are they? Planets? If so, how in creation did they form so quickly?"

Abna did not answer. He went over to the telescope, adjusted it, then peered intently through the lens. There was a puzzled look on his face as he motioned the Amazon over.

"They're planets!" she exclaimed, removing her gaze from the eyepiece. "They can't have suddenly become visible just because the *Ultra* is moving slowly toward them: they've leaped out of nowhere and been created. Why?"

"I don't know," Abna answered simply. "Maybe something to do with the destruction of Kolb... There's only one way to find out. Go and see!"

With that he went over to the control board and pulled the speed lever into its second notch, his eyes—and the Amazon's—set meanwhile on that fantastically glittering diamond formation in the depths of the Milky Way.

ABOUT THE AUTHOR

British writer **JOHN RUSSELL FEARN** was born near Manchester, England, in 1908. As a child he devoured the science fiction of Wells and Verne, and was a voracious reader of the Boys' Story Papers. He was also fascinated by the cinema, and first broke into print in 1931 with a series of articles in *Film Weekly*.

He then quickly sold his first novel, *The Intelligence Gigantic*, to the American magazine, *Amazing Stories*. Over the next fifteen years, writing under several pseudonyms, Fearn became one of the most prolific contributors to all of the leading US science fiction pulps, including such legendary publications as *Astounding Stories*, *Startling Stories*, *Thrilling Wonder Stories*, and *Weird Tales*.

During the late 1940s he diversified into writing novels for the UK market, and also created his famous superwoman character, The Golden Amazon, for the prestigious Canadian magazine, the Toronto *Star Weekly*. In the early 1950s in the UK, his fifty-two novels as "Vargo Statten" were bestsellers, most notably his novelization of the film, *Creature from the Black Lagoon*.

Apart from science fiction, he had equal success with westerns, romances, and detective fiction, writing an amazing total of 180 novels—most of them in a period of just ten years—before his early death in 1960. His work has been translated into nine languages, and continues to be reprinted and read worldwide.

MORE BORGO PRESS TITLES BY
JOHN RUSSELL FEARN

THE ANJANI SERIES

The Gold of Akada: A Jungle Adventure Novel
Anjani the Mighty: A Lost Race Novel

THE BLACK MARIA SERIES

Black Maria, M.A.: A Classic Crime Novel
The Murdered Schoolgirl: A Classic Crime Novel
One Remained Seated: A Classic Crime Novel
Thy Arm Alone: A Classic Crime Novel
Death in Silhouette: A Classic Crime Novel

THE HERBERT THE DINOSAUR SERIES

A Thing of the Past
The Genial Dinosaur

OTHER BOOKS

1,000-Year Voyage: A Science Fiction Novel
Account Settled: A Science Fiction Mystery
Bury the Hatchet: A Crime Tale
A Case for Brutus Lloyd: A Science Fiction Mystery
The Crimson Rambler: A Crime Novel
Don't Touch Me: A Crime Novel
Dynasty of the Small: Classic Science Fiction Stories
The Empty Coffins: A Mystery of Horror
The Fourth Door: A Mystery Novel
From Afar: A Science Fiction Mystery
Fugitive of Time: A Classic Science Fiction Novel
The G-Bomb: A Science Fiction Novel
Here and Now: A Science Fiction Novel
Into the Unknown: A Science Fiction Tale
Last Conflict: Classic Science Fiction Stories

Legacy from Sirius: A Classic Science Fiction Novel
The Man from Hell: Classic Science Fiction Stories
The Man Who Was Not: A Crime Novel
Manton's World: A Classic Science Fiction Novel
Moon Magic: A Novel of Romance (as Elizabeth Rutland)
One Way Out: A Crime Novel (with Philip Harbottle)
Pattern of Murder: A Classic Crime Novel
Reflected Glory: A Dr. Castle Classic Crime Novel
Robbery Without Violence: Two Science Fiction Crime Stories
Rule of the Brains: Classic Science Fiction Stories
Shattering Glass: A Crime Novel
The Silvered Cage: A Scientific Murder Mystery
Slaves of Ijax: A Science Fiction Novel
Something from Mercury: Classic Science Fiction Stories
The Space Warp: A Science Fiction Novel
The Time Trap: A Science Fiction Novel
Valley of Pretenders: Classic Science Fiction Stories
Vision Sinister: A Scientific Detective Thriller
Voice of the Conqueror: A Classic Science Fiction Novel
What Happened to Hammond? A Scientific Mystery
Within That Room!: A Classic Crime Novel
World Without Chance: Classic Science Fiction Stories